A Chance for Lara

Last Chance Brides, Book 3

by Cat Cahill

Copyright

---

1. http://www.catcahill.com/

Chapter One

Last Chance, Nebraska - June 1895

Two more steps and the saddlebag would be within her reach.

Lara Cummings glanced toward the porch. The scrawny, squirrelly man with the derby hat and the mustache as narrow as a thistle stem, stood uncertainly halfway between his horse and the porch steps. He clutched a sheet of paper to his chest—and Lara *desperately* wanted to know what was written upon it.

She took another step. The man's horse shuffled, but made no noise. She halted for a moment, just in case the creature changed its mind.

Up on the porch, her sister Belle stood terrified while her cousin Josie, only three months away from giving birth, leveled a shotgun at the fellow with the paper.

"Now see here, Mrs. Thomas," the man in the hat said. "I've only come to deliver this to your husband and your brother—"

"I own this ranch as much as they do," Josie said in a clipped voice as one of her loyal dogs, Noel, sauntered out from the house to stand at her side.

"Yes, yes, ma'am. I'm certain you do. May I deliver this to you then?" He held out the paper like some sort of peace offering.

"I know what it is, and I don't want it."

The man gave a nervous chuckle. "I fear I never introduced myself. I'm James Snyder, of the Lincoln Bank. You may recall that your husband and brother took out a mortgage two years ago—"

"And I said, I don't want it." That shotgun held steady.

Lara drew her eyes back to the matter at hand—getting to that saddlebag. While Mr. Snyder tried—and continued to fail—to give Josie that sheet of paper, Lara took the last step toward the horse.

"Good girl," she said under her breath as the mare dropped her mouth to nibble at the little bits of brown grass that remained amid the dusty dirt. Silently, looking quickly toward Mr. Snyder to ensure he was still engaged with Josie, Lara reached out and pulled a sheath of papers from the open saddlebag.

Holding them to her side, hidden amid her skirts, she carefully stepped away from the horse and took a wide berth back to the porch. She grabbed hold of one of the posts and pulled herself up onto the wooden slats just as Josie's husband Arlen emerged from the house, his own shotgun at his side and the other two dogs, Holly and Shepherd, at his heels. The dogs were all white, just like their mama, Christmas, had been.

Lara clutched the papers behind her back as she slipped into place next to Belle.

"What did you do?" her younger sister hissed, not daring to take her eyes off the situation at hand.

And a situation it was too, now that Arlen raised his own shotgun.

"Not a thing," Lara said, but she gestured toward her back.

"Lara!" Belle's eyes were wide, and Lara shook her head in a silent message to her sister to keep this to herself.

"You have thirty seconds to see yourself back to that horse, Mr. Snyder, before I see fit to send these dogs here after you." Arlen nodded toward the dogs.

Lara bit her lip to keep from laughing. Noel, Shep, and Holly would just as soon lick him to death than bite him, though they were big enough to look intimidating to anyone who didn't know better.

Mr. Snyder's gaze flicked to the dogs. "That's not necessary, sir. I only want to—"

"One," Josie said.

"Two." Arlen reached down to pet Shep.

"I'll just . . . I'll leave this here then. You folks come see me in town. All right?" Mr. Snyder leaned down to drop the paper to the ground.

"Nine," Arlen intoned.

Belle gripped Lara's hand as Mr. Snyder scurried to his horse. He didn't notice that the papers were gone from his saddlebag.

Arlen continued counting, but a small cloud of dust from near the front gate drew Lara's attention away from the man scrambling to mount the impatient mare. The dust cleared some to reveal another man on horseback. Lara drew in a breath. Surely Mr. Snyder hadn't brought along someone else.

But no. This man wasn't dressed in the nice suit that Mr. Snyder wore. He had on a far more practical hat and wore clothes that didn't mind the dirt. He sat at ease on his horse as he watched the proceedings in front of the house.

"Twenty-one." Arlen sounded bored now, as if he were disappointed he didn't get to take a shot at Mr. Snyder.

"You folks have a fine day," Mr. Snyder said in a strained voice as he turned his horse around and headed for the gate. He paused and said something to the man waiting outside the fence, and then, thankfully, he was on his way.

Belle let go of Lara's hand as their cousin and her husband lowered their shotguns. With a deep, exhausted sigh, Josie leaned against the wall of the house. Belle scurried over to take the shotgun from her.

"Why don't you sit down inside?" Arlen said, his face a map of worries as he watched his wife. "I'll see what this other fellow wants."

"Probably work," Josie said as she brushed away Belle's proffered arm. "Lara, will you round up the girls to come help with supper?"

Lara nodded. Josie and Arlen's two daughters were off playing with a litter of new kittens in the barn. The door shut behind Belle and Josie, but the dogs kept their watchful place on the porch beside Arlen. Lara took one step toward the stairs, but stopped as the man who was now inside the gate dismounted his horse.

Fetching the girls could wait a moment, she decided, as the man moved with casual ease toward the porch. Lara's curiosity often got the better of her, but who *wouldn't* want to know who this stranger was?

"Good afternoon, sir," the man said. "Miss." He tipped his hat to Lara, and she caught a glimpse of eyes as dark as his hair.

"I assume you don't work for the Lincoln Bank?" Arlen said, that shotgun at his side like an unspoken threat.

The man's eyes found the shotgun before he looked back to Arlen. "No, sir, I do not. I only just rode up as the other fellow was getting on his horse. My name's Mitchell King, and I'm looking for work." He spoke in a low, careful voice, as if he thought through his words before giving them life.

"Well, you've come to the wrong part of Nebraska, Mr. King," Arlen replied. "There's not a soul around these parts that could pay you right now."

If Mr. King was surprised by those words, he didn't show it. Lara thought it too bad they couldn't afford to hire him on. He looked as though he knew his way around a ranch, with that easy way he carried himself. It seemed as if there wasn't a situation that could possibly unnerve him. Not to mention those broad shoulders and that strong jaw—

Lara swallowed hard as she clasped the papers to her side. What was she doing, thinking of this stranger in that way? One might think she'd never seen a man before, and here she was mooning over him as her thirteen-year-old cousin might have done.

He glanced at her again, and the blood rushed to her ears as she offered him what she hoped was a friendly smile. When he finally looked back at Arlen, the breath rushed out of her body. It was a good thing they didn't have work at the ranch for him, otherwise Lara might never feel at ease again.

Mr. King shifted his stance as he looked from Arlen off to the west pastures and then back at Arlen again. "Well, you're in luck, then. Looks like you need someone and I don't require pay."

Chapter Two

The words were out of Mitchell's mouth before he could take them back.

No pay.

Was that really what he'd just offered?

He resisted the urge to glance at the pretty redheaded girl who stood off to the side on the porch, fixing his gaze instead on the ranch owner and his dogs.

The man gave him a puzzled look, and Mitchell didn't blame him one bit. No other fool had ever likely ridden up and offered to work his ranch for free.

"You don't require pay," the man repeated Mitchell's words back to him.

Mitchell swallowed dust. This was, what, his sixth or seventh stop? And not a one was able to pay. So maybe this was the way instead. "That's what I said. Look, sir—"

"Thomas," the man interrupted. "Arlen Thomas. This here is my wife's cousin, Miss Cummings." He gestured at the young woman Arlen had tried so hard not to stare at. But his eyes found her again now, and she held his gaze in a way most would think was bold, curiosity written all over her face as she clutched a sheath of papers to her stomach with both hands.

"Pleased to meet you, Miss Cummings," he said.

Her face turned nearly as red as her hair and he had to bite the inside of his cheek to keep from grinning, and for a moment he thought he'd work for scraps and a bed in a horse stall just to see her blush like that again.

He dragged his eyes away from Miss Cummings, mentally berating himself. If he was to work here, he doubted he'd be here long if Thomas thought he was paying any sort of questionable attention to his kin.

"I've traveled days across this prairie, looking for work. Not a soul has money, and I understand that. All I seek is a bed and three meals a day." He paused, thinking maybe even that was out of reach for these folks. "Most folks can't spare a scrap of food these days, and I see you've got young ones . . ." He trailed off as two girls clambered up to the porch, the youngest one staring at him as if she'd never seen a stranger before.

It was a hopeless request. No one could take on an extra mouth. He ought to have gone south from Denver instead of north. But what was done was done, and now he'd need to find a place to bed down for the night so he could start again in the morning.

The thought of riding away left him with a hollow sort of feeling as he glanced at the redhead again. She was watching him, not a lick of shyness or embarrassment in her face. She was the most curious woman Mitchell had ever seen, and the thought of not getting to know her hurt almost as much as the hunger pangs gripping his stomach.

"Arlen," she said. "Perhaps this man could help while Josie prepares for the baby."

When Mitchell had ridden up, there was a woman with a shotgun—a woman who was clearly expecting.

Thomas nodded, seeming to consider her words. "Might be we can help you out. We have a bunkhouse. And while we don't have a lot of food, what we've got won't let you go hungry." He paused. "You sure you're all right working without pay? Every other hand we had hired on here left because we couldn't afford to pay them any longer."

"In other times, I wouldn't be. But these days are different."

"All right then. I'll need to run it by my wife and her brother, but consider yourself hired. Bunkhouse is over there." Thomas pointed across the yard, out toward the barn, stable, and another building Mitchell assumed was the bunkhouse.

"We'll have dinner on at six-thirty," Miss Cummings said, the two girls crowding beside her as Thomas excused himself to head inside the house. "Beef stew with potatoes. No carrots or onions, though, I'm afraid."

"And pudding, Lara. Don't forget the pudding," the older girl said. "I made it myself." She blushed when she said that, and Mitchell smiled.

"In that case, I'm sure it's good," he replied, hoping they wouldn't hear the grumble of his stomach at the mere mention of food. They could have served dead grass and roasted pinecones, and he'd probably gobble it up as hungry as he was.

"We'll see you then." Miss Cummings smiled at him, shifting those curious papers to her side.

"Miss Cummings," he said just as she turned to go inside after the younger girls. "Thank you. For helping me. I won't forget it."

"Of course." He might have been imagining it, but he thought her cheeks had turned pink again.

"Please tell Mr. Thomas he won't regret hiring me on."

She nodded. "I'll tell him."

And then she was gone. He stood alone out there in front of the house, the expanse of the ranch stretching for miles around him.

They wouldn't regret it, Mitchell determined. It wouldn't be like the other places he'd scared up work in Colorado before he'd landed in Denver. He was alone, and it was high time he accepted it. If he did, he could be at ease here. Far away from Denver and the trouble he'd left back there.

Because no one here in Last Chance, Nebraska knew him.

Mitchell smiled wryly at the thought of the town's name as he led Trip to the stable. *Last Chance*. It was fitting, in a way, given how long a stretch he'd gone without work—and without a decent meal.

Yet it felt more like a second chance than a last chance. A second chance to settle in somewhere, to work hard instead of taking the easy way out, to live a respectable sort of life.

He halted Trip just outside the stable to drop his satchel, saddlebags, and blankets in the dusty, brown grass. Trip's reins loose in his hands, Mitchell paused before leading him inside. He breathed deeply, the dry air filling his lungs as he took in the vastness of the prairie, from the bluffs that rose far off to the south to the road that seemed to go on forever.

No one knew him here. It was a fresh start.

And that was exactly what he needed.

Chapter Three

One more person in the kitchen would likely send Josie into labor far too early, particularly with Hannah and Dot bickering nonstop and the dogs underfoot. Leaving Belle to sort that mess out, Lara excused herself to collect the washing that hung behind the house.

Lara made quick work of gathering the linens, shaking them out to remove the ever-present dust, and folding them neatly. Basket at her side, she took the long way around the front of the house. It was to avoid the chaos in the kitchen, she told herself.

And maybe to catch a glimpse of Mr. King, but she would never admit that.

The barn door stood open, and his things lay in a neat heap just outside the door. Lara paused, worrying her lip with her teeth. It would be a nice gesture to carry them into the bunkhouse for him. And she'd do just about anything to make him want to stay here. Josie was so worn out, trying to keep up with the ranch chores that George and Arlen couldn't do alone.

They desperately needed Mr. King's help so Josie could finally rest.

Lara set her basket down and began to gather Mr. King's bags and blankets. It would give her a good excuse to check in on the bunkhouse, ensure everything was clean and that there were linens on the bed.

His bags weren't heavy, and as she carried them to the bunkhouse, Lara wondered how a man could travel with so little. When she and Belle came to the ranch from their parents' home in Ohio two and a half years ago, they'd each brought a full steamer trunk and a carpetbag. And even then, they'd had to leave some things behind.

The air inside the bunkhouse was still and stale. Setting down her load, Lara crossed to the windows and opened them. Even if the wind kicked up and blew a little dust inside, it would be worth it for the fresh air.

Turning and brushing her hands together, Lara surveyed the room. It was in satisfactory shape for a place that hadn't been used in nearly a year. She ought to tell him she brought his things over here, lest he think someone wandered by and ran off with them. Should they launder those blankets for him? At the very least, they probably needed airing out and a good beating to remove the dust.

She picked them up, considered them, and then put them back down. It was better to ask first. For all she knew, Mr. King found comfort in the scent of horseflesh and dirt. Lara smiled at the ridiculous thought. She was about to move toward the door when the corner of something—was that a photograph?—sticking out from his satchel caught her eye.

Without thinking, she knelt and reached for it. But the second her fingers touched the edge, she paused.

What was she doing?

It was one thing to sneak those terrible *Mortgage Due!* notices from the bank man's saddle bag, but something else entirely to extract this photo from the satchel of a perfectly nice man who was to work for the ranch.

Yet her fingers still held on to the corner of the photo. What would one little peek hurt? It wasn't as if she'd take the picture—it wasn't there to cause harm to her neighbors, after all, like those bank notices. And it wasn't as if she'd opened the bag and gone pawing through it. It was sticking out, like a fallen acorn just waiting for a squirrel.

No. The word blossomed in her mind, only for the roaring wave of curiosity to drown it out. It was as if she *had* to know. And if she didn't, the desire to know would sit like an itchy thing just under her skin.

This is why you left home.

This is why Belle feels like she can't trust you.

This is how you ran off every possible suitor who came calling.

"That wasn't me, that was the drought!" Lara said to herself.

"What was the drought?" Mr. King's low, unhurried voice sounded from above her.

Lara ripped her hand away from the photo and jumped to her feet. "Mr. King, I— Nothing. I was thinking aloud." She clasped her hands together and prayed he wouldn't question why she'd been hovering over his satchel like a thief.

That particular prayer went unanswered. Or perhaps God decided that now was the perfect time to teach her a lesson.

"Might I ask what you were looking for in my bag?" Mr. King said, glancing from her to the satchel on the floor.

"I . . ." Lara followed this gaze. The bit of photograph still protruded from it, taunting her. Who was in the photo? She shook her head just slightly, trying to clear it. What a thing to wonder right now!

"Miss Cummings?" He'd crossed his arms and his look of mild concern had transformed into the beginnings of a scowl. "I don't take kindly to thievery."

"Oh, no!" Words finally seemed to make their way to her mouth at the same time a traitorous warmth crept into her cheeks. Mama had always said honesty was the best when presented with the opportunity for a lie, so Lara bit down her embarrassment and opted for the truth. "I'm sorry. I was merely curious about that photograph. I shouldn't have pried. Please don't leave."

He stared at her a moment as if debating whether her explanation was satisfactory. His jaw worked as his dark eyes traced her face. Lara fought the urge to squirm. It was almost laughable, how much taller he was. His future wife would have to get used to craning her neck to speak to him or kiss him.

Oh, good heavens! Why was she thinking about kissing?

Certain her face was the same shade as a summer tomato by this point, Lara fought hard not to look away. Perhaps he'd think she was only embarrassed because she was caught almost pulling that photograph from his satchel.

And not because she was imagining those likely well-muscled arms wrapping themselves around her and pulling her to that broad chest—

"I'm not leaving. Not just yet. But I expect a degree of privacy, Miss Cummings." Mr. King paused, dropping his arms to his sides. "Besides, you might not like what you find when you go prying in a man's things."

Well, if that didn't just make her even more curious about what might be inside his satchel. Lara swallowed, trying to push that thought away. "I apologize again, Mr. King. I'll leave you to get settled. Please let us know if you'd like those blankets laundered, or if you need fresh linens." Her face flamed again. It seemed the hospitable thing to say, but now all she could think was that she'd mentioned bed linens in front of this man who she'd only imagined kissing a moment ago.

He chuckled. But whether at her words or her embarrassment, she didn't know. "I'll be sure to do that." He scooped up his bags, that little yellowed corner of the photograph still peeking out from the satchel. She had to yank her eyes away from it.

"Oughtn't you get back up to the house? Some might consider your presence here scandalous." Amusement lurked at the corners of his lips as Lara fought to keep from blushing again—and she realized that was what he'd *wanted* to happen.

She straightened, pressing her shoulders back. If he wanted to play a game, she could certainly hold her own. "It's only scandalous if you make it so, Mr. King."

He had no response to that, but he didn't look away. He shifted his satchel on his shoulder. Her eyes fell to the open flap again. That photo was like a beacon, drawing her attention over and over—and she *had* to know. "Who is in that photograph?"

The words lingered between them, her driving need to know everything out in the open. It wasn't any of her concern,

Lara knew that well enough. But perhaps he'd tell her, and then she could walk away with that incurable desire for knowledge soothed for the moment.

He held her gaze, and she wondered how it was possible to have eyes that shade, so dark they nearly blended into his pupils. Then those eyes crinkled around the edges as he shook his head and smiled.

"My horse. Trip."

Lara blinked at him. The man had paid for a photo of his *horse*? Then again, she ought not be surprised. If she could, Josie would have photographs of her dogs and cats displayed in the house.

"Satisfied?" he asked, still smiling in a way that made Lara question whether he'd told her the truth—and wondering if he could see past her question to her insatiable curiosity about everything. Or whether he was playing the game again.

"Perhaps," she said lightly before moving toward the door. She glanced back at him before sliding outside to retrieve the laundry. "Perhaps not."

Chapter Four

Six-thirty couldn't arrive fast enough.

Mitchell forced himself to walk at a normal pace toward the house, even though every part of him wished to run as fast as he could toward the food awaiting him inside.

He climbed the steps to the porch and paused outside the door. Should he knock? He'd never been the only ranch hand around before.

Better to knock than to walk right in and offend them, he decided. He barely knocked once when the door opened. The younger of the two girls he'd seen on the porch when he arrived stood there. She gave him a cherub-like grin.

"Come in, Mr. King. Mama was asking about you."

"I hope I'm not late." That would be impossible. He'd watched the seconds on his pocket watch like a man who'd never tasted food.

"You're not." Mrs. Thomas gripped the edge of the kitchen doorframe, a towel in her hand and her face flushed from exertion. Seeing the woman look as if she could do with a good, long sit in a chair made Mitchell even more grateful he'd taken this job. He couldn't imagine Mrs. Thomas outside chasing down calves and repairing fence line in her state.

The scents that wafted through the air made Mitchell want to sprint straight to the kitchen and start eating the stew straight from the pot. But he forced himself to remain planted in the parlor, where the girl who had answered the door and her older sister stared at him with eyes wider than dinner platters.

"These are my daughters Hannah and Dot," Mrs. Thomas said, gesturing at each girl in turn. The older one, Hannah, blushed, while Dot gave him a big grin. "Girls, will you show Mr. Thomas to the dining table while I help Belle?"

Dot immediately took hold of his hand and began to pull him toward a doorway off to the left, chattering nonstop about Shep, Holly, and Noel, who Mitchell eventually figured out were the dogs.

"They're outside right now. Mama says they have to stay outside when we have company eating with us," Dot finished. "You should sit there." She pointed at the nearest chair.

It didn't feel right sitting when no one else was in the room, but to Mitchell's great relief, Arlen Thomas appeared in the doorway with another man Mitchell guessed was his brother-in-law just behind him.

"George Cummings," the other man said, reaching out a hand. He was the spitting image of his sister, but his brown hair sported streaks of gray. "Glad you agreed to stay on. Now maybe we can convince Josie to sit down more often."

"Good luck with that," Arlen said with a strained smile. Worries sat obvious and heavy on his shoulders, and Mitchell felt an instant kinship with the man. God above knew he had his own parcel of worries, but at least he didn't have a family to feed in the middle of a drought.

Mrs. Thomas and a younger, blonde woman, who Mitchell also remembered from his arrival, bustled into the dining room with plates of bread and a tureen of stew. There was no water at the table, but the blonde woman poured each person a mug of bitter-smelling coffee.

Mitchell resisted the urge to pour the entire contents of his mug down his throat immediately. He distracted himself with wondering where the curious and somewhat impudent Miss Cummings had gone.

"Where is Lara?" the older girl, Hannah, asked as if she were reading his mind.

"I'm here," came a breathless, familiar voice from behind Mitchell.

She moved quickly around the table and took the empty seat across from him, wearing a different dress of some green striped material that set off her hair and eyes to such a degree that Mitchell had trouble not staring.

She's nosy and potentially a thief. Well, perhaps not the latter, but the thought helped him regain his senses and accept the bowl of stew that Cummings passed to him. Besides, even if she was, he was the last person to judge a thief.

The meal was more chunks of beef and potato than any sort of actual stew. It was a given, considering the lack of water, and Mitchell didn't mind one bit. It looked—and smelled—far more edible than anything else he'd eaten in the past few weeks.

The very moment Mrs. Thomas lowered her spoon to her bowl, he dove in. And he didn't stop until every bite was gone.

The beef was tough and the potatoes were past their prime, but Mitchell barely noticed.

When he looked up, he found Miss Cummings watching him, her blue eyes alight with amusement as she chewed.

"Would you care for more, Mr. King?" the blonde woman at Miss Cummings's side asked.

"Please." He passed his bowl across the table and she ladled him some more of the meat and potatoes. "Thank you, Miss . . . ?" He trailed off, realizing he'd not yet been introduced to her.

"Cummings," the redheaded Miss Cummings supplied. "This is my sister, Belle."

Belle Cummings gave him a tentative smile. "We're glad you're here, Mr. King," she said in her soft voice, although something about the way she spoke made him question whether she believed her own words.

"Papa, will you tell us about the water machine again?" Dot asked.

Arlen smiled indulgently at the little girl. "I will indeed. As soon as we can scare up that last dollar, we'll have it come here." He launched into how he'd seen it drill deep into the ground, searching for water in town and out on the James farm. "It's a miracle, is what it is."

"It's science," his wife said.

As they argued good-naturedly about whether the machine was a God-given miracle or science—with Mr. Cummings chiming in that it was likely a bit of each—Mitchell found himself distracted by the woman across from him.

Miss Cummings had finished her meal and was listening to the discussion with what seemed like rapt attention. A curl of rust-colored hair had fallen from her upswept style, and she brushed it away absentmindedly. A sprinkling of freckles dotted her nose and cheeks and Mitchell smiled at their presence. A woman with freckles wasn't one who much minded fashion or fretted about being outdoors.

A dusting of short, white hairs rested on the shoulder of her striped dress, and Mitchell pondered where they might have come from before realizing it had to be from one of the dogs. So this woman who clearly didn't mind sticking her nose into his personal items loved dogs and spending time outside.

She caught him staring at her in that exact moment. He should look away, pretend he hadn't been staring and letting thoughts of her consume his mind. But questions bloomed in her eyes, and he remembered her little grin and the way she'd said *"Perhaps"* back in the bunkhouse when he asked her if she'd learned enough about him.

And he didn't look away.

Her cheeks pinkened just a bit—which he'd admit made him want to look at her more often—but she didn't draw her gaze away either.

As much as he shouldn't be interested, given that his livelihood depended upon remaining in the good graces of her family, Mitchell couldn't help but want to know everything about her. What made her so bold? Where were her parents? Was there a man who came around to pay visits to her?

There should be a man courting her. Maybe that would drive some sense back into his head.

"Perhaps now Lara will tell us what she took from Mr. Snyder's saddlebags earlier," Mrs. Thomas said. She folded her hands over her stomach and sat back, her eyebrows raised in expectation.

"I . . ." Miss Cummings's eyes widened as everyone at the table looked to her.

"You shouldn't have. I told you so," her sister said in a whisper.

Miss Cummings drew her lower lip between her teeth. She didn't deny the accusation.

This was certainly interesting. So Miss Cummings had a penchant for going through others' belongings, and not just his. Mitchell wasn't certain if he was relieved or disappointed. He hardly carried anything that would implicate the misdeeds of his past, but her actions had made him wonder if she hadn't suspected him of being more than a ranch hand. That was, of course, when he wasn't hoping her curiosity had been sparked simply by an interest in him.

Finally, Miss Cummings sighed. "I took the mortgage notices. For . . . everyone. That he hadn't yet delivered, of course. I didn't mean to take them. I only wanted to look, but when I saw what they were and I thought about how upset everyone would be to receive one, well . . ."

Mitchell laughed.

He couldn't help it. It was the least devious theft he'd ever heard of.

The entire table turned to look at him, and he stopped abruptly. Miss Cummings gave him a little smile as she bit her lip.

"I apologize. I was only imagining that bank man arriving at the next ranch to find his notices missing," he said.

"I rather like that thought," Mrs. Thomas said with a laugh of her own. "Serves him right."

Arlen and George smiled too, and the tension in the room seemed to disappear. Only Miss Cummings's sister remained unamused. She leaned over and whispered something in Miss Cummings's ear.

"Your mother would wish me to admonish you," Mrs. Thomas said, still smiling. "But I'm afraid I can't. Please don't tell her."

"Oh, I won't," Miss Cummings said fervently.

After enjoying Hannah's pudding, Mitchell made his way back to the bunkhouse, feeling lighter than he had in a long time. Memories of his own family flickered through his mind. He'd like to think they would have been a lot like the Thomas and Cummings family . . . if they'd lived.

But the thought didn't sully his mood, as it normally did. Instead, he found himself drifting off to sleep that night with images of his own family around a dining table—and thoughts of a pretty, mischievous redhaired woman.

He'd have to watch himself around her. One blink of those clear blue eyes and he'd tell her secrets he'd never planned to tell a soul.

Chapter Five

"Only one piece." Lara rubbed Murray's nose as the gelding tried to snuffle his way toward more of the molasses and oat treat in her skirt pocket. "Once we have water again, I'll make you an entire batch, all right?"

Murray looked at her through doleful eyes, and she laughed. He'd been her favorite horse since she'd arrived in Last Chance, and she was thankful each day they didn't have to sell him off as they had with so many of the other horses. Not that there were many left who could afford to buy a horse.

Lara gave Murray one last scratch on the nose before moving to the next stall, where Mr. King's horse had been pressing his nose as far around the stall as possible. "How about you, sir? Would you like a bite?"

The horse snorted as if saying yes. Lara grinned and extracted the last bit of the cookie. She held it out and the horse gobbled it up.

"Are you looking for something of mine?" Mr. King's low voice sent goosebumps racing up her arms.

Lara forced herself not to leap back from his horse. She was doing nothing wrong. "Indeed, I am not. Unless you consider offering your horse a cookie something nefarious."

"A cookie?" He arched one of those eyebrows again as he removed his hat, and Lara's pulse quickened.

Get a hold of yourself. She'd never been so flustered around a handsome man before. It was ridiculous that she should be with Mr. King, considering how he clearly didn't much care for her.

"Yes," she said primly, running her hand over the horse's velvety nose. "A horse cookie. It's made of molasses and oats. Sometimes I add bits of apple or carrot. When we have those . . ." She was rambling. Lara forced herself to stop speaking, which was much easier to do when she looked at the horse instead of Mr. King's half-amused, half-suspicious expression.

"A horse cookie," he repeated. "Now there's something I've never heard of in all my years."

"Well, now you have. And your horse here liked it."

"Trip," he said. When she glanced at him, he added, "The horse's name is Trip."

She remembered that now from the bunkhouse. "So Trip enjoys cookies and being photographed." Lara winced the second the words were out of her mouth. Why was she reminding him of her interest in his photograph?

But to her surprise, Mr. King laughed. "That photograph wasn't of Trip, although I'm sure you figured as much." He paused. "It's a photo of my parents."

The words were like water to a parched throat, slaking her curiosity for at least the time being. Lara stepped back from Trip and looked at Mr. King again. His face was serious now, and if she wasn't wrong, she thought she saw a trace of sadness in the way his shoulders dropped.

Guilt crept up her spine.

"I'm sorry." Lara clasped her hands together, hoping this wouldn't turn out the way it had so many times before. "I shouldn't have tried to look at that photograph. It's . . . I . . ." How could she possibly explain the all-consuming need to *know* things?

"Your curiosity gets the best of you," he said, those dark eyes watching her.

Lara blinked. No one had ever understood, at least not immediately. Josie had come the closest, seemingly accepting the facet of Lara's personality that got her into the most trouble. "It's my most terrible shortcoming. It's why I left home and came here." She stopped speaking and bit down on her lip. She hadn't shared that fact with anyone beyond the family here at the ranch.

He nodded, appearing to be unfazed at this confession, and Lara felt immediately that her secret was safe with him. "We all have our own reckonings to face."

She searched his eyes, that curiosity roaring to life in the back of her mind. What sort of reckoning did Mr. King expect to face?

He didn't look away, even as she searched for his secrets as if they might reveal themselves in those dark eyes.

Finally, he drew his gaze toward his horse, and Lara's breath flooded her lungs. How did this man have the power to make her stop breathing?

"Shortcoming though it may be, I have to admit that I admired the way you filched those mortgage notices from that banker," he said with a chuckle, although his eyes remained on Trip.

Something about his warm laugh made her relax. "No one's ever found amusement in my . . . inability to leave well enough alone." Her family here was more tolerant of the scrapes she found herself in—far more so than her own parents had been. Yet no one had ever laughed like Mr. King.

"I doubt there's been much to laugh about around here in a while," he said, raising a hand to stroke Trip's neck but turning his eyes toward her.

"You'd be right about that." The lack of rain had kept her cousins up night after night. She and Belle often heard them talking into the wee hours of the morning, discussing options—some of which she'd like to forget had ever been mentioned.

"I imagine this place was quite the operation a few years ago." Mr. King leaned against the stall, his arm resting on top of the door.

Lara gave him a wistful smile. "I wish you could have seen it as I did when I first came here. Green grass, as far as I could see in all directions. The North Platte was wide and full and fast, not that sad trickle of mud it is now. The ranch had so much livestock that George used to worry they wouldn't find enough men to round them up come fall. They'd hire on so many ranch hands that some of them had to set up tents out beside the bunkhouse. Josie refused to let Belle and me walk by there." That past annoyance was now a distant memory.

"It's a miracle they've kept the place going," Mr. King said.

"It hasn't been easy." Lara paused. Was this the season when things would turn around for them? First, the water machine came to town. And now they'd hired on Mr. King. "But I have great hope for the future. Thank you for offering to work here. Before you, and before the water drill, I'd feared we might lose everything."

"That won't happen." Mr. King spoke as if he could know what would occur in the future.

"It is still a possibility," she admitted. "If we can't come up with that last dollar. Or if the machine can't find water here and the rains don't come this summer." As much as she hated to speak those thoughts out loud, it was no use pretending that everything was suddenly fixed. Or that Mr. King could count on true employment here in the future.

He shook his head and then leveled that unnerving gaze at her. "This place was your second chance, right?"

Lara swallowed. Why had she told him about having to leave Ohio? He was essentially a stranger. And yet, she didn't recant her words. Something compelled her to continue to be honest with him. "It was. It is."

Mr. King nodded, as if he were considering her words. His eyes were shadowed, as if there were something deep inside him that he didn't yet feel he could trust her with. And then, without a word, he reached for the hat he'd hung over the top of one of the stall posts. He placed it on his head, cocking it at an angle she was certain he knew made him look particularly roguish.

"It's my last chance too."

And then he was gone, leaving her to ponder his words in the cool darkness of the stable.

By the time Lara got hold of herself and began to walk back toward the house, she knew three things for certain.

One, Mr. King was a man with a secret.

Two, she yearned so badly to know exactly how dangerous that secret was.

And three, if she had any sense at all, she'd stay far away from him.

Chapter Six

Days passed in a blur of ranch work, easy conversation, and Mitchell's desperate attempts to keep his mind off Miss Cummings. But the latter wasn't easy, considering she was often outside, feeding the remaining chickens, playing with the dogs, sweeping the porch, and entertaining her cousins. Mitchell was almost grateful for the frequent presence of her sister, who watched him with suspicion. He didn't know what he'd done to deserve to land on her bad side, but the younger Miss Cummings didn't much care for him at all.

It was just as well, though. Between her and learning that Arlen used to work as a sheriff, Mitchell kept his brief conversations with the redhaired Miss Cummings to a minimum. Yet that didn't stop her from entering his dreams at night or waltzing into the corners of his consciousness when he had a moment or two to himself during the day.

The only reason he could figure that she wasn't already married up was that obnoxious sense of curiosity she possessed.

Once he understood it wasn't malevolent, Mitchell found it charming. He'd caught her devouring a newspaper from Omaha late one afternoon, soaking up the words as if she couldn't get enough. Another time, he found her interrogating a hapless fellow who'd simply stopped at the ranch for directions. By the time the man left, Miss Cummings knew his business, his place of birth, the names of every member of his family, and the general geography of St. Louis where the man had grown up. All of this she relayed with glee to the family at supper.

Those suppers had come to be Mitchell's favorite part of the day. He rarely spoke, instead preferring to enmesh himself in the fabric of this family. Miss Cummings's chatter, the men's discussion of business, Mrs. Thomas's daughters' thoughts on whether the baby would be a boy or a girl, the impatient way the dogs—who were now allowed back into the dining room—would lay under the table, hoping for a scrap to fall.

The familiarity of it was comforting and something he'd craved for so long without realizing what he'd been missing. It was like the ranch had put back a piece of his soul that he'd lost long ago, back when his parents died, back before he'd found himself in a world of trouble in Denver, back before he'd made the decision between freedom and loyalty.

That last thought came to him as he sat back in his chair after finishing another meal of beef—butchered from the ranch's own meager stock and carefully parceled out to last—and old potatoes. He closed his eyes for a second as the words ran through his mind again.

Freedom or loyalty.

He'd been on the move for so many months, scratching out an existence that barely kept him alive, that he hadn't had much time to think on the decision he'd made late last fall. Guilt pinched at the corners of his mind from time to time, but he'd pushed it away.

But now that he had time to think, out here with the blue sky and the promise of water on the way, he knew he'd done the right thing. It had felt wrong at the time—almost selfish—betraying Clarkson like that to save his own hide. Even though the man had crossed a line that Mitchell would never have followed him over. But it had been the right choice to make—the *only* choice.

What Clarkson would never know was that Mitchell had saved his life.

"Mr. King?" A sweet, soft voice said his name, drawing him back into the present.

Miss Cummings's face was drawn up in concern as the others around her engaged in conversation. "Are you all right?"

The past was the past, and that's where it ought to stay. Thinking on it would do no good for the future. Mitchell nodded.

Next to him, Dot, the Thomases' younger daughter stood up. "Hannah and I have something to say."

The table quieted, and all eyes went to the little girl, who grinned as if she was holding back a secret bigger than Christmas. She looked to Mrs. Thomas, who nodded at her.

"We're the reason there weren't eggs for breakfast this morning. Or yesterday." Dot's round face looked sheepish, but that smile didn't leave her face.

"This had better be good," Arlen said. "My stomach missed those eggs."

"Oh, it is, Daddy! Just wait. Hannah and I, we went into town with Belle and Lara, and we sold the eggs to Miss Hollie at the diner. She asked us how much we wanted for them, and we told her a dollar." Dot looked at Hannah, who extracted a few coins from her dress pocket and set them on the table.

"It's for the water machine," Hannah said in her quiet voice.

"The last dollar," Miss Cummings said from across the table, excitement bursting from her in what was possibly the most beautiful smile Mitchell had ever seen.

As the table erupted into joyful conversation, Miss Cummings turned that radiant smile onto Mitchell. "You were right," she said.

The salvation of the ranch was hardly a done deal, but Mitchell would take that sweet, happy look she gave him any time. His hand itched to reach across the table and cover hers, but he kept it firmly planted in his lap. Instead, he reveled in the glow in her eyes, the smile she shared only with him, and the animated chatter around them.

When he told her they wouldn't lose the ranch, he meant it. And he would tell her again and again if she needed to hear it. He would do everything in his power to keep this family here—and his job on this land. Including suggesting to the girls that they might sell something to raise the last of the money.

"Thank you for the idea, Mr. King."

He dragged his eyes away to Dot, who was looking up at him. "It was merely a thought. You and your sister made it happen."

She smiled at him before turning to answer a question from her mother. When Mitchell looked back up, Miss Cummings still watched him, her head tilted just so and her eyes full of questions.

Mitchell didn't attempt to answer any of them. Instead, he sat back and relished the feel of her eyes on him.

He couldn't have her, not if he wanted to remain here. But that rational thought seemed to fly to the edges of his mind when she looked at him.

Treading on the edge of danger was what he'd always been good at, after all.

#####

The water finder arrived with just the right amount of cacophony. Birds flew from the drooping trees, and everyone on the ranch streamed to the yard in front of the house when it came in on the wagon.

Hart Chapman, who Mitchell had heard plenty about but hadn't yet met, jumped down from one wagon, while his partner, Ambrose Young, drove the machine to the middle of the yard. The men introduced themselves as Miss Cummings's sister and little Dot peered at the machine, all three dogs winding around their legs.

After shaking hands with both Chapman and Young, Mitchell stepped back with George and Arlen while Mrs. Thomas retreated to the porch to watch. He glanced out to the road. Miss Cummings would be sad to miss this.

"I wish Lara and Hannah were back," Arlen said, shaking the dust from his hat as he put Mitchell's thoughts into words.

"They should be soon," Mitchell replied. It didn't occur to him that he should have kept that to himself until Arlen glanced at him with a questioning raise to his brow. "Considering they left so early."

It must have been enough, because Arlen looked away, back to the water finder that the men were now preparing to drive to the rear of the house where a line of underground water was suspected to be, given the maps that had been drawn up after the first few findings of water.

In truth, Mitchell seemed to be aware of Miss Cummings's whereabouts all the time. Instead of listening to the sensible part of himself that said to leave well enough alone with her, he found himself even more aware of her actions, her words, and, of course, each and every time she looked at him.

The wagon with the water finder trundled around the house, and they trailed after it, no one wanting to miss the first drilling into the ground.

Just as he rounded the corner of the house, Mitchell heard thunder. He paused.

No, that wasn't thunder.

It was hoofbeats.

And whoever it was, they were coming fast.

"Arlen." The man turned when Mitchell said his name. Mitchell pointed at the road, where dust was beginning to form not too far off.

"I'll see what this is," Arlen called back to George and the men with the wagons. "You go on and get started." Arlen glanced at Mitchell, who nodded. If this was trouble, he wasn't sending the man in by himself.

They strode away from the group, back toward the front of the house as the hoofbeats and the dust cloud grew closer. Mrs.

Thomas stood from her seat on the porch, her hand shading her eyes.

"It's Hannah," she said after a moment.

And just then, the dust cleared enough to show a girl flying up to the gate on a horse.

Mitchell's shoulders sagged as he relaxed the hand he'd instinctively placed over the revolver at his side. Trouble wasn't at their door.

But something had made the girl come galloping back home. And—he looked past where she drew up at the gate—without Miss Cummings.

"She's alone," he said to Arlen. A hundred different scenarios flooded his mind. Miss Cummings, thrown from her horse and gravely injured. Set upon by men with ill intentions. Lost somewhere in town.

"Hannah!" Arlen ran to the open gate where Hannah hadn't yet dismounted. Mitchell raced to catch up to him.

"What happened? Are you hurt? Where's Lara?" Arlen flung the questions at his daughter one after the other as he reached up to help her dismount.

But the girl stayed put on her horse. She was covered in dust and her hair hung loosely in her face from where it had fallen out of the braided style she usually wore. "I'm fine, but you must come with me. Please, Lara needs your help."

Bile rose up Mitchell's throat. Lara—Miss Cummings—was hurt. "How bad is it?" He had to know.

The girl looked at him, confused for a half a moment before shaking her head. "No, she's fine. It's another lady. One we happened upon on the way back from town. Her wagon overturned and her horse ran off. She's hurt really bad, and Lara stayed with her."

Mitchell closed his eyes for just a second. Lara was fine. She wasn't hurt. She was still here.

"King!"

His eyes flew open to find Arlen staring at him. "The horses." It was a guess. He hadn't heard a thing the man had said.

Arlen narrowed his eyes just slightly, and for a moment, Mitchell was certain the former sheriff could see right through him—from his unrelenting attraction to Lara to his close brush with prison in Denver. "You all right to go out? I can get George."

Mitchell shook his head. "I'm fine. I'll get the horses if you're getting the wagon." He strode toward the corral before Arlen changed his mind. His heart hadn't slowed a bit since Hannah had come riding up alone. He needed to see Lara. Make sure she was whole and uninjured.

And he needed to stop thinking of her as *Lara*. Because that sort of familiarity could lead to nothing good.

Well, he thought as he led Trip and another of the horses from the corral, it *would* be good until her cousins ran him off their land with shotguns. How worth it would that be, when he'd finally found the place that felt the most like home?

He could have a brief moment with Lara—or he could have a lifetime at the Cummings-Thomas Ranch, with Lara just out of reach.

There was no in between.

Chapter Seven

Lara had never seen a more welcome sight than a dust-covered Hannah returning with two equally dust-covered men driving a wagon. She'd assumed from a distance that both Arlen and George had come, but as they drew closer, it became clear that the man she thought was George was actually Mr. King.

Her heart thumped as she continued to wind the shawl Hannah had offered up around the injured woman's mangled leg.

"Is that them?" The woman's little boy—who'd proudly told Lara that he was five years old—pointed down the road to the horses and wagon.

"It is," Lara said, tying off the shawl as best she could. "Help is coming." She looked up at Mrs. White. "This isn't the best, but it should help stop the bleeding until the doctor arrives."

"Thank you." The woman, who was maybe around thirty years old, raised herself to lean back on her hands. If they had been closer to the overturned wagon, she could have leaned against that, but Lara didn't dare try to move her without help.

"You're an angel. I'm sorry, I know you told me your name, but I've forgotten."

Lara smiled at her. "It's quite all right."

"It's Lara," the little boy said. "Lara Cummings."

"*Miss* Cummings, Joseph. Don't go forgetting your manners," his mother corrected him.

"Lara is just fine." Lara stood and brushed the dust from her hands as the horses drew up.

"Then you must call me Isabel."

"Isabel. That's a beautiful name, don't you think so, Joseph?" Lara said, mostly to distract the little boy who was looking at where the blood had already begun to seep through the shawl.

"Nah," he said, and Lara grinned.

"Hannah told us what happened," Arlen said as he strode from the wagon, Mr. King at his side while Hannah hung back and held onto the horses' lines.

Mr. King knelt in the dirt. He tilted his hat to Isabel before asking, "May I?"

She nodded, and Lara watched as Mr. King peered under the edge of the shawl. "Looks to be broken pretty good," he said as he tightened the cloth again. "But nothing the doc can't fix up." He directed those last words to Isabel, and she gave him a wavering smile.

Lara couldn't imagine the pain the poor woman was in. "How are we getting her into the wagon?"

"Very carefully," Arlen said.

Lara stood back out of the way with little Joseph, telling him the tale of the time she climbed a tree when she was a child and fell right out onto the ground to distract him from his mother's grimaces as Mr. King and Arlen lifted her from the ground.

"Was there blood?" the little boy asked, his attention fully on her now.

"Not a drop," she said. "But I broke my arm. And I got into a world of trouble because I was trying to see over into the neighbor's fields."

Joseph's eyes widened. "Why would you want to do that?"

Lara glanced over toward the wagon, where the men were gently working to lift Isabel into the wagon box. She looked back down at Joseph. "Well, I was certain they were spies."

"Were they?" He nearly breathed the question out, and Lara smiled. She couldn't dash his hopes.

"They spoke a language I'd never heard before, had many visitors to their farm late into the night, and never invited anyone over for tea or dinner. What do you think?"

"Oh, they were!" She could almost see the boy's imagination running wild.

"Lara, can you settle her in while we pull some items from their wagon?" Arlen called.

Lara took Joseph's hand. "Why don't you come with me? You can sit by your mama."

The boy skipped by her side and she lifted him up into the wagon box before climbing in herself. She took off and wound up her own shawl to create a pillow for Isabel's head, and made sure she was positioned in a way that would cause the least amount of jolting to her injured leg.

"Arlen's looking for the purse with your money," Mr. King said when he came back to the wagon. "But I found your jewelry box and this carving." He handed the items over the side to Lara.

"Thank you," Isabel said. "My late husband made that little owl for me. We couldn't bring much with us when we left home, and that's one of the few things I have left from him." She paused. "I lost the house and the land to the bank."

Lara's heart ached. She gave her the carved wooden owl to hold while she secured the jewelry box and tried to blink away the tears that had gathered in the corners of her eyes.

"How is the boy?" Mr. King asked quietly, his eyes moving from Joseph to Lara.

"Fine," she said. "I told him a story of spies and breaking my arm, and that proved to be quite the distraction."

Mr. King lifted his eyebrows as he draped his hands over the edge of the wagon box. "Sounds exciting. I think I'd like to hear that story someday."

Lara bit down on her lip to keep from smiling too broadly as she checked the jewelry box. "I must admit it's one of my far-too-curious-for-my-own-good scrapes."

"Then I definitely need to hear about it."

She looked up at him. How was she supposed to keep hold of her senses when he looked at her with those startling eyes and that devilish grin? She wanted so badly to know more about him—and especially about whatever secret he was keeping. She'd buried herself in learning about anything else for the past two weeks to distract herself from all the questions that brimmed in her mind about Mr. King. Why, she'd even cornered some poor farmer for an hour one afternoon, when all he wanted to know was how far he was from Grand Platte.

Lara bit down harder on her lip to keep the questions from surfacing. Where had he come from? What had happened to his family? What had he done before arriving in Last Chance? Why did she feel both drawn to him and afraid of what went unsaid? Why did it seem as if he walked the edge of something entirely lawless and wild?

"Where did you receive medical training?" Something had to come out, and that seemed the most innocuous question to ask.

"I didn't." He pulled off a glove and ran a hand through his hair as she waited for him to continue.

When he said nothing, she pressed a bit more. "Then how did you know what to look for with Mrs. White's wounds?"

He slapped the empty glove against his other hand. "My mother."

"Your mother was a physician?" Lara couldn't decide if she was more surprised or amazed.

"Oh, no." Mr. King shook his head. "Although she could have been. She was talented beyond any measure with diagnosing and treating illnesses and injuries. Our little town didn't have a doctor, and she was the closest thing to medical treatment most folks could get."

Lara thought for a moment. It was far more impressive that his mother hadn't been trained as a physician. "And she taught you?"

He shrugged. "My brother had more interest than I did, but I picked up a few things here and there."

"Is he older or younger, your brother? Do you have any other siblings?" She couldn't stop the questions now. They tumbled out like a waterfall from a mountain ledge.

Mr. King's jaw twitched. He tugged on the glove. Whether or not he was going to answer, Lara didn't know, as just at that moment Arlen arrived with the purse Isabel had asked for.

"Ready to get moving? We'll still need to send for the doctor, and I want to get back to that water machine," he said after reassuring Isabel that they would return later to gather up the broken wagon and everything left in it.

Mr. King nodded, and with a quick look back at Lara, he made his way to the front of the wagon.

"I'll ride back here and keep her comfortable," Lara said to her cousin, although her mind was still on Mr. King.

He consumed her every thought on the ride home. She hadn't expected him to have a way with treating injuries. What else was there to uncover?

Chapter Eight

"No, Mr. Mitchell, you're supposed to stay *behind* the well till Dot faints." Joseph planted his hands on his hips.

"I told you, I don't want to faint. I want to fight!" Dot held up an imaginary gun and aimed it at the well that held only a little muddy water.

"Girls are supposed to faint," Joseph said. "It's a fact."

"It's no such thing!" Dot's face screwed up red. "Just ask my mama."

Mitchell held up a hand. He could just imagine Mrs. Thomas coming out here to give little Joseph a lesson on what women were good at. Just trying to get the woman to sit down for the good of her baby was hard enough when she insisted she could still rope livestock and carry heavy bales of old, dry hay. "Let's not do that. How about you allow Dot to do as she wishes? And I'll stay behind the well this time. All right?"

Joseph kicked the dirt. "All right." He raced to the back porch, paused for half a second, and then bellowed, "I know you spies are out there! Come on out or I'll shoot you!"

Mitchell bit the inside of his cheek to keep from laughing at the little boy's exuberance.

"Who are you going to shoot?" Lara paused at the back porch, Hart Chapman and Ambrose Young with her.

"The spies. Ssh, Miss Lara. You'll mess it all up!"

Lara nodded gravely and covered her mouth with her hand. She and the two men beside her watched with amusement as Joseph flew from the back porch out into the brown grass.

Mitchell waited for Dot to make her stand—and then run away laughing as Joseph fired his pretend bullets at her—before he rose from behind the well.

Joseph paused in his play. "You're *supposed* to—"

"What kind of spy would I be if I just let you get away with capturing me?"

Joseph thought on that for second before pretending to fire a gun at Mitchell. "Got you, you dirty spy!"

Mitchell clutched at his heart and tumbled to the ground. A cloud of dust rose around him, and he was pretty sure he swallowed some of it. The things one endured to entertain children.

"Joseph, can you please resurrect Mr. King? These gentlemen need to get on with the drilling," Lara said.

"Come on, get up." Joseph pulled at his hand, but Mitchell continued to play dead. "Miss Lara, he's not getting up."

Through the slivers of sight between his eyelids, Mitchell saw Lara peering down at him.

"Hmm," she said, arms crossed. "I imagine that if you start tickling his side, he'll awaken, good as new."

Before Mitchell could react, Joseph dove in and began tickling him. Mitchell laughed and jumped up, catching the boy under his arm and holding him upside down.

"That worked, Miss Lara," Joseph said as his hair skimmed the ground.

She laughed, as did the other men, and Mitchell brought the boy to the porch to dump him gently onto the wooden slats.

"Why don't you go check on your mama?" he said. Joseph nodded and ran inside.

Chapman and his partner were already making their way to the machine when Mitchell joined Lara.

"You have a way with him," she said. "And with Dot." If he wasn't mistaken, she looked at him with something akin to admiration shining in her eyes.

Mitchell pulled off his hat and ran his hand through his hair. "That's what comes with being the eldest child."

She said nothing, which Mitchell presumed was likely a first for her. But he could hear the questions bouncing around her mind anyway. He'd avoided them yesterday, when she'd asked about his family out there by the overturned wagon. But he'd grown to know her well enough that the question would come again.

He might as well get it over with as quickly as possible. "Four siblings. One brother and three sisters, all younger. What did the doc say about Mrs. White?"

She blinked at him, and he knew she wanted more. But he wasn't inclined to speak on the past right now—or ever. And thankfully, she let it go.

"He apologized for not making it by yesterday, but said you and Josie did well setting the leg. So long as it doesn't take on gangrene, it should heal well. He said to keep it clean and to change the bandages frequently."

Mitchell nodded. "She's something else, your cousin." Mrs. Thomas had gone right to work the second they'd brought Mrs. White into the girls' bedroom. He'd assisted, but she'd done the bulk of the work.

"I know." A smile played at the corners of Lara's mouth. "She's night and day from my mama, but according to my grandmother, she's exactly like my Aunt Vivi. And my Aunt Vivi isn't anyone you'd want to mess with."

"I might say the same about you, Lara."

Her cheeks went pink and she looked away, toward the water drill—but only for a second. Then those blue eyes were back on him, narrowed just slightly as a smile played upon her face. "I don't recall giving you permission to call me by my Christian name, Mr. King."

"I don't generally ask permission for much of anything."

Her eyebrows shot up, and those little spots of pink in her cheeks turned red. It had been a risky sort of thing to say, but he'd say it again to catch her off-guard like this.

And to Lara's credit, she didn't back down. Instead, she took a step forward, and then another, until she was so close he thought he could feel her breath against his neck. "That's an awfully interesting statement, *Mr. King*. One might wonder what other kinds of things you didn't request permission to do."

His heart thumped like it had taken on a life of its own. He was treading on a very dangerous line on multiple levels. And yet he didn't back away. He didn't apologize. Instead, he let a smile turn up his lips. "Well, *Lara*. I suppose you'll have to get to know me better to find out."

She lifted her chin and a vision of his hand resting against her jaw, pulling her closer and closer until there was no space left between them, roared to life inside his mind. Mitchell's fingers flexed involuntarily as he forced them to stay put against his sides.

"I'll accept that challenge," she said, smiling so prettily that he nearly forgot how badly he needed her *not* to get to know him better.

What had he done?

She dipped her chin and stepped back, and the space between them finally allowed Mitchell to draw in a breath.

"I've already figured out one thing about you," she said.

His stomach lurched upward, imagining all the bits of his past she could have somehow dug up.

Lara poked a finger at his chest. "You aren't the hardened, rough man you'd like everyone to think you are."

"I'm not?" He shifted his stance, wondering where exactly she was going with this.

She shook her head. "You've a heart in there, Mr. King. A soft heart that loves children, your family, and your horse. I know there's a lot more to you than that, but I think that at the end of the day, your heart rules everything you do."

And with that, she turned and made her way toward the water drill—leaving Mitchell to stand there, feeling more dumbfounded than he'd ever been in his life.

Chapter Nine

Stars shone above, bright and numerous in the inky sky with no moon. Lara breathed in a lungful of the dry air. Sometimes she wished for rain so badly she thought she could feel it against her skin.

But when she opened her eyes, it was still as arid as it had been for the last two years. Who knew that merely six months after her arrival in Last Chance that everything would have gone so wrong? She and Belle had arrived here, hopeful and full of dreams. And now she prayed each day for something as simple as rain.

Something moved in the darkness, out near where the water drill sat, paused for the night. Lara's heart jumped into her throat. It was a man, that much was clear from his silhouette. Whoever it was stopped too, and she could feel his eyes on her.

And she knew it was him.

She moved down the steps, drawing her shawl more tightly around her shoulders. "What are you doing out here?" she asked Mr. King.

"I could ask you the same." He didn't wear a hat, and in the darkness, she could just make out the way his hair hung over his forehead. He pushed it aside, his eyes on her.

"I couldn't sleep," she said truthfully.

"Me either."

They stood in silence for a moment, both looking at the hulking shape of the water drill.

Lara swallowed, and then put her gravest fear into words. "What if it doesn't find water?"

"It will," he said.

She looked up at him. "How can you be so certain?"

He shrugged. "It's the only thing I have to hold on to."

"It isn't the only thing." She let the words linger in the air as she ran the toe of her half-done-up boot over the ground. *You have me.* That was too much to say aloud, too forward, too . . . *everything.* Instead, she added, "Arlen and George have come to depend upon you."

"I'm not part of this family, Lara," he said, and shivers raced up her spine at his insistent use of her given name. "If there are too many mouths to feed, I'm the first to go."

Lara pressed her lips together. The thought of him leaving was impossible. "They'll find water."

She could feel his eyes on her, and when she looked up, he was smiling. "See, that's better, right?" he asked. "Doesn't that make you feel better? It sure does for me."

Lara returned his smile. "When Belle and I came here, there was plenty of water. Everything was green and the fall was brilliant. During winter, there was plenty of snow. And then . . ." She shrugged. "It dried up."

"Why didn't you go back?" he asked. "To your parents? Surely that would have been easier than sticking it out here."

"It's . . . well." Lara shifted and pretended to adjust her shawl. "My opportunities in Ohio were limited."

"Opportunities?"

"Marriage," she said, cringing a little at her bluntness. But it was the truth. "No one much cared to marry the girl who asked too many questions."

"Only questions?"

When she looked up at Mr. King, he was still smiling at her. He knew. He might not know exactly how much trouble she'd found herself in, rifling through one fellow's private papers and discussing another's business affairs with a newspaperman, but he *knew*.

And could she dare think that he liked it?

"No," she said, and left it at that.

His smile grew even wider. "Surely your sister wasn't so . . . forthright in investigating her suitors?"

Lara laughed. Belle would *never* consider peeking in a man's satchel. "No, certainly not. But I fear my actions as the older sister reflected upon her too. And so we both came here, somewhere no one knew us, in the hopes of starting again."

She didn't need to add that it hadn't worked out so well for either of them, considering neither had found herself married. The drought had ruined all of that, and most of the eligible men had fled town.

"It's not any easier back home. Papa is struggling, and they have our little brothers to feed. If Belle and I returned, it would make it that much harder on them," she said.

Mr. King nodded. "Times are hard everywhere."

"Why couldn't you sleep, Mr. King?"

"Mitchell."

She blinked at him.

"You can call me Mitchell."

He was trying to distract her. "You didn't answer my question."

"I was thinking about the water too." He didn't look at her when he said this.

Lara tilted her head. "You said you were certain they would find water."

Mr. King—it felt far too dangerous to think of him as Mitchell—didn't answer.

Something else was bothering him. What was it? She plucked a question from the hundred that had lurched their way into her mind. It was on the tip of her tongue . . . but should she ask?

This was exactly the sort of thing that had convinced her parents to send her and Belle off to live with their cousins here in Nebraska. A real lady would bite her tongue. She'd let a man decide when and if he needed to tell her what sat in the deepest recesses of his mind.

But Lara was, apparently, no real lady. Besides, he'd essentially challenged her to learn more about him. And he'd been impressed—or at least amused—by her curiosity, not angered.

"Were you thinking of your family?" There. It was out. Now it was up to him to answer or not.

His chest rose and fell, and then, finally, he looked at her. "Some. But mostly other things."

Other things. Knowing him, he probably said that to stir her mind into a frenzy. She settled on another question. "Were you thinking on what happened before you arrived here?"

His eyes were definitely on her now, slightly narrowed, and his smile turned into something serious. "What do you know of my time before I came to Last Chance?"

"I . . . I don't." That intense look in his eyes had sent her mind tumbling over itself. This was that *something* she'd seen in him before. That dark, hidden part that made her want to run away and run to him at the exact same time.

Lara swallowed and straightened her shoulders. If she wanted to know, this was no time to back down. "Something happened to you before you came here. I imagine that whatever it is, it sits heavily on your mind." It wasn't a question, but an invitation to share more. It felt wrong to ask more directly.

His gaze didn't shift even a fraction of an inch. Lara held perfectly still, not looking away. "You're right, in a way. It's always in the back of my mind, but it isn't anything that happened *to* me."

Which only meant it was something he did.

Perhaps this should scare her. But Mr. King . . . Mitchell was right about one thing. Lara was very much like Josie and her Aunt Vivi—she didn't scare easily.

Not that she could summon the thought of being scared of him to begin with. His eyes softened as she held his gaze, and a lock of hair that desperately needed cutting fell across his forehead again. What she really wanted to do was to ensconce herself into his arms.

Instead, she reached for his hand.

The wild thought that she was being too bold flared across her mind the second her fingertips touched his, but she couldn't pull back now.

She didn't *want* to pull back now.

He paused and stiffened for just a moment, and then he relaxed, wrapping his hand securely around hers.

Lara lost track of how long they stood like that, hands entwined, eyes on the water drill, and stars twinkling overhead.

The night was so still and silent that when a voice interrupted it, Lara nearly leapt straight up into the air.

"Hello? Lara, is that you?"

Mitchell dropped her hand immediately as they both turned back toward the house. And there was Belle, just in front of the steps. Lara couldn't see her expression, but unless Belle had only just arrived, she most certainly had seen Lara's hand in Mitchell's.

"Miss Cummings." Mitchell nodded at Belle, his voice perfectly even. "I'll bid you both good night."

He held on to Lara's gaze for just a split second longer than was proper before disappearing around the house.

Belle's eyes were immediately on Lara's. "What was that?"

Belle never raised her voice, but Lara had known her too long to miss the reprimand in her sister's quiet words. There was no use denying it. And Lara didn't want to—not to Belle at least. "You know very well what that was." She gave Belle a smile. "It's fine. I think . . ." What did she think? She wasn't in love . . . was she? "He's a good man," she finished lamely.

Belle made a noise deep in her throat. "I don't know, Lara. I want to think he is, but there's something about him. Please tell me you've seen it too."

Lara pressed her lips together as she wrapped her arms around herself, the shawl snug around her shoulders. "Nothing more than I imagine any man carries."

But it *was* something more. She chewed on her lip as she thought about Mitchell's response to her question. If it wasn't something that had happened to him, it was something he'd done.

What had he done?

She swallowed hard before forcing a smile upon her face for Belle. "We came here to find good men to marry, didn't we?"

Belle frowned. "You wish to marry him?"

Yes. No! For goodness's sake, she'd only just questioned whether she could even be in love with him. Why on earth would she be thinking of marriage? "I'm enjoying myself, that's all. There are so few men left here, Belle. And when a good one of the right age shows up and seems interested in me, why shouldn't I enjoy that?"

Belle twisted her hands together before rubbing them up and down her arms. Lara opened her shawl, inviting her sister to come closer. Belle didn't hesitate, and together they huddled under the shawl.

"I only ask that you be careful. I don't want you to lose your heart to him only to be disappointed." Belle paused, her eyes on the water drill. "He seems the sort who might go running when the past catches up with him."

Lara shivered, but she covered it with a laugh. "You know me. If there is something nefarious in his past, I'll uncover it. Likely to my own detriment."

Belle leaned her head against Lara's. "If you even get that far before Arlen and George go chasing him off."

Lara grinned. "Please don't breathe a word to them."

"Of course not," Belle said. "Now if only a handsome cowboy would come riding up for me."

The sisters laughed together as they strode back to the house, and by the time Lara climbed into bed, her fears had dissipated, leaving only the memory of Mitchell's hand around hers and a pair of dark eyes with no desire to look anywhere else but at her.

Chapter Ten

The ricochet of the water drill was just barely noticeable this far out past the ranch, but it was a comfortable reminder of what was to come.

Mitchell urged Trip over a rise in the land, keeping his eyes trained on the horizon for signs of the few cattle the ranch had left. By some miracle, there had been one calf born in the spring, but it was a daily struggle to keep the rest alive. The calf and his mama were kept closer to the ranch to ensure their survival, but the rest . . . Mitchell only hoped he didn't happen on any that were dead.

The water drill thumped away, digging in a new place after the first was unsuccessful. Mr. Chapman had been optimistic about this second choice, and so Mitchell remained optimistic too.

With no cattle in sight, his mind wandered back to where it usually did these days—to a place much more rewarding than the old thoughts of Clarkson, Denver, and all of the poor choices of the past.

He smiled at nothing as Lara entered his mind. He'd essentially promised her that Chapman would find water. If that happened, the ranch would be saved. They'd rebuild the herd, pay off the past-due interest on the mortgage, and Mitchell himself would be paid.

And once he had money, he could put it away to build something of his own. A house, maybe. With a small plot of land. Some place where he could firmly put the past behind him and have a wife and a family.

Lara's image danced into his mind again. He knew she'd come here looking to marry. And he certainly hadn't imagined the way she looked at him—or how she'd reached for his hand last night.

Was it possible that she might consider—

A scream rent the air, drowning out the thud of the water drill. Mitchell pulled up hard, forcing Trip to a stop. He looked this way and that across the land.

The scream came again. This time he could tell the direction. He aimed Trip at a clump of trees that sat at the edge of the road.

When he arrived, he peered through the trees. The foliage was sparse, given the lack of rain, but there was still enough to make it impossible to see past the first two or three trees. Mitchell slid off Trip silently. He looped the reins around the nearest tree and pulled the revolver from his holster.

All he could figure was that some nefarious sort had overtaken a woman on the road. If that was the case, they'd be on the road, behind the copse of trees, and he could catch the man unaware if he came at him from within the trees rather than from the road.

So when Mitchell rounded a stalwart pine to find a tall man with his hand clamped over the mouth of a woman he'd backed up against a dead trunk, it caught him by surprise.

And when he realized the woman had red hair, falling from its pins, sheer anger replaced the surprise.

Wait. If he jumped in right now before assessing the situation, he could get them both killed. The man was tall—taller than even Mitchell himself—with a battered hat and a tan-colored coat that looked far too warm for the day. Hair the shade of straw showed from beneath the hat and a dirty hand clamped over Lara's mouth. He wore a pistol on his hip. That shade of hair, and that height, reminded him of something, but he didn't know what.

"Don't you give me trouble," the man said in a voice that sounded as if it had been raked over rocks.

Mitchell forced himself to loosen his grip on the revolver. Clenching the thing wouldn't do anything but cramp up his hand, rendering him incapable of acting.

With his other hand, the blond man grabbed hold of the back of Lara's neck and forced her away from the tree, toward the road. She kicked out at him, just barely missing his leg as he laughed.

Mitchell didn't hesitate another second. He strode forward as silently as possible. When he was just behind the man, he reached out with his left hand and yanked him backward.

The man yelped as he stumbled. His grip on Lara slackened, and he dropped his right hand from her mouth to reach for his revolver.

But Mitchell held up his own weapon and aimed it squarely at the man. "Take your hands off her."

The man's hand stopped in mid-air. He glanced between Lara and Mitchell. Then, in a sudden motion, he pushed Lara forward and ran off into the trees toward the road.

Mitchell leaped forward, catching Lara against him. He holstered the pistol and grabbed hold of her arms. "Are you all right? Did he hurt you?"

She shook her head, her face brave but her body shaking. Without thinking, Mitchell pulled her to him, desperate to make her feel safe. "It's all right. I've got you. He's gone."

She nodded against his shoulder before sagging into him. His hand ran a circle over her back, and slowly, she stopped shaking.

Lara leaned back in his embrace, just far enough to look up at him. Not a tear stained her face, but fear still lurked in her eyes. He didn't dare let go of her.

"You're safe," he said.

She nodded. "Thank you." Her sweet, brave voice held an edge he'd never heard before—and one he hoped never to hear again.

A rage worked up inside him, directed at the man who'd scared her so badly. What right did he have to come here, onto her family's land, and terrify her?

Lara turned just slightly in his arms, her eyes going to the road the trees concealed.

"He's long gone by now," Mitchell said. "Did he say anything to you?"

She shook her head.

"He was likely a drifter, desperate with the times. He won't be back."

Her gaze slid back to him and she nodded. "I've never felt afraid here before."

"As you shouldn't." He lifted his hand from her back and pushed a strand of hair away from her face. "Nothing bad will happen to you so long as I have breath in my body. I promise you that, Lara Cummings."

She shuddered again, but not from fear this time. Mitchell dropped his hand to her cheek, letting his fingers trace the line of her jaw. Her eyes fluttered shut and she leaned into him, entirely trusting.

That trust filled him up, made him want to be worthy of it. He'd told her the truth. He would fight anything bad that came her way. He would keep her safe if it was the last thing he ever did.

When he dropped his hand to her shoulder, she opened her eyes and looked up at him. He thought he could see the questions blooming in her mind.

His Lara, forever curious.

He barely had time to question his own thought—what made him think she was his?—when she asked the first question.

"Why?"

At first he thought she was asking why he'd think she was his, and his words caught in his throat.

"Why do you care so much about this ranch?" She paused. "About me?"

He didn't know how to answer the second question. So he answered the first with bare honesty. "It feels like home. I haven't had a home—not a real one—in years."

She nodded. "I understand that." She didn't elaborate, but she didn't need to. Mitchell knew she felt the same about this place as he did.

"We ought to get you back up to the house," he said. And as much as he didn't want to, he let her go.

But she held on to his hand as he led her back through the trees to Trip. He helped her onto his horse and walked beside her as they headed back toward home.

Lara told him of how much she enjoyed walking the ranch, and that's what she'd been doing when that man had appeared and pushed her back into the trees.

Mitchell furrowed his brow as he listened. Something about the man had been oddly familiar. But try as he might, he couldn't place him.

Perhaps he had him confused with someone else. That was the most likely answer. After all, this was Last Chance, Nebraska. A place where Mitchell had never stepped foot before.

He'd ride into town and alert the sheriff. The man was probably long gone, but it wouldn't hurt to ensure others knew to watch for him.

He glanced up at Lara. She was safe, and that was all that mattered. He'd probably remember why that man looked so familiar in a day or two, and then he'd laugh over the coincidence.

Or so he hoped.

Chapter Eleven

The well water clung stubbornly to its brown shade, no matter how many times Lara strained it through the cheesecloth. Well, it would have to do. What she'd give to wash dishes—or drink!—water that looked and tasted clean and fresh.

But for now, it was mud-tinged water with minuscule pieces of dirt. As she scrubbed the breakfast dishes with it, she felt Josie's eyes on her.

Her cousin sat at the kitchen table, the hem she was fighting on a gown for the baby forgotten in front of her as Noel whined for attention. Lara smiled at her as she dried her hands. "You ought to ask Belle to do that. She could have that hemmed in half the time that you or I could."

Josie scowled at the tiny gown. She reached down and scratched Noel behind the ears. "Isabel already offered, but I insisted I should do it myself."

"You ought to let her. I'm certain she's grown exceedingly bored just sitting there and healing." Lara set the towel down and pulled out the chair next to Josie.

"I wish I'd kept Hannah and Dot's baby clothing." Josie ran a finger over the cloth.

"Well, then you wouldn't have had room for Belle and me." Lara smiled at her cousin. This baby was a surprise, coming years after Dot, and years after Josie and Arlen had assumed there would be no more babies.

"I'm sorry your time here hasn't been what you'd hoped." Josie folded her hands over her stomach and eyed Lara.

Lara knew that look. There was more meaning to Josie's words than she'd let on. "It's been perfectly good. You know that," she said carefully as she mentally ran through how she could be in trouble. She hadn't asked any questions that were too nosy today, hadn't rifled through the mail that Arlen had brought home yesterday, and hadn't even taken the catalog Belle had brought home from town before anyone else could read it. "Is this about the man who grabbed me yesterday? Because I'm fine, Josie. I promise that I am."

"I know. You're a strong woman," Josie said. "It isn't that. Well, perhaps a little . . ." She shook her head. "I'm sorry. It isn't like me not to be direct. You came here to find a good man to marry, and I know that hasn't gone as planned. I just want you to know that I see the way you look at Mr. King—and how he watches you."

Lara caught her breath. Belle wouldn't have gone against her word, but Lara should have known that Josie would catch on. If she wanted to let Mitchell go—

"And I think it could be good for you both. I haven't said anything to the men yet. Goodness knows they'd chase him off the ranch without so much as asking for an explanation. I'll speak to them if it becomes necessary. In the meantime, I trust you to keep your head about you."

Lara nodded, not daring to speak.

"He's a man with sorrow in his past, Lara. I can see that in his eyes. So however this goes, be gentle with him." Josie pushed herself up to standing and gathered the gown.

Lara rose to provide support to her cousin, but Josie waved her off.

Isabel's laugh sounded from the girls' bedroom, followed immediately by George's. Lara raised her eyebrows as she looked at Josie.

"I may as well go take Isabel up on her offer." Josie gave Lara a mischievous grin. "After all, we can't expect George to entertain her all the time. And then I'd better lie down before I hear from Arlen about how I'm not letting myself get enough rest. You'd think sleeping all night would be enough, but not according to him." She shook her head. "The girls took Joseph and the other two dogs out to watch the water drill. Would you mind checking in on them? I think Joseph and Dot together might be too much for Hannah sometimes."

Lara promised she would. She made quick work of the rest of the dishes and left the water to use again later in the day. When George scurried out of Isabel's room, he nodded to her, not stopping to answer the questions she was dying to ask of him as he escaped out the front door. Lara smiled at herself.

Outside, the sun promised another rainless day as Mr. Chapman and Mr. Young prepared to put the drill into motion again. The children sat quietly nearby, and Lara caught snippets of a story Hannah was telling that seemed to have both Dot and Joseph enraptured.

Out here, with the wind gently blowing through the trees and the voices of children, Lara felt Mitchell was right. Nothing could hurt her—or any of them here. That man on the road was a strange occurrence. Nothing that would happen again.

But still, she ran her hands over her arms when she thought of the way he'd pressed his hand over her mouth when she screamed. She'd never forget how his lank hair hung in his pale eyes, or how he'd growled at her to come with him.

She didn't know what he wanted with her, and she didn't care to think on it too long. It was best left alone. Nothing had happened. And she was fine.

Lara busied herself for the remainder of the morning, checking in on Josie and Isabel, penning a letter home to Mama and Papa with Belle, and ensuring the children stayed out of trouble.

Lunch was a quick affair, with Josie dutifully staying in bed and the men hard at work repairing the barn. Belle and Lara wrapped up bread and cheese and beef, and Lara set out to deliver it to the men.

But when she reached the barn, only Mitchell was there, fitting a new board into place where an old one had split and fallen loose.

"Are you hungry?" She held out one of the meals wrapped in brown paper.

He pulled off his gloves and climbed down from the ladder he'd stood upon. "Starving."

Lara grinned as he took an enormous bite from the bread. "Where are Arlen and George?" She held up the other two packages.

"Off checking on cattle," he said after he swallowed a mouthful of cheese. He glanced up at the barn. "I'll ride out there with you."

Lara tried to hide her smile. "Don't you have to finish the barn?"

"Not much left to do."

"All right. I'll saddle the horses while you eat." She forced herself to walk to the corral even though she felt like skipping. A ride alongside Mitchell sounded like a wonderful way to spend an hour or two. Maybe she'd finally get him to tell her more about his family. Or maybe he'd simply look at her with those eyes she thought could see right through her. Perhaps they'd stop somewhere, and he'd touch her face again and then she'd close her eyes—

Murray's nuzzle against her face brought Lara back to the present. She saddled the two horses as quickly as possible and returned to where she'd left Mitchell outside the barn.

"Which way did they go?" she asked.

"South." He eyed Murray. "Do you need help?"

"I . . ." Too late, she realized there was no stool out here to assist with mounting the horse. "I can go back in—"

She hadn't finished her thought when he'd rounded the horse and wrapped two strong hands around her waist. Lara fought against a gasp as he picked her up, as easily as if she were a kitten, and set her on the saddle.

"Thank— Thank you," she finally managed to say.

He gave her a devilish grin. "Don't tell me you ride sidesaddle."

Lara glanced down at the saddle, where she was sitting to one side as she tried to push the feel of his hands on her waist from her mind. Then she gave him her own mischievous grin. "I grew up on a farm. Of course I don't ride sidesaddle."

And then, awkwardly, she bunched her skirts up and swung her leg over the other side of the saddle. Then she urged the horse forward, leaving Mitchell behind to scramble up onto his own horse to catch up.

Chapter Twelve

This must be what heaven felt like.

Riding across an open field, sky as blue as a sapphire, the perfect amount of breeze, and the most beautiful woman in the world at his side.

Well, Mitchell reflected, if it truly were heaven, there would be an occasional rain.

But that was all right by him. He wasn't ready to leave this earth just yet, and he'd endure an unending drought just to see the way Lara looked at him—as if he were incapable of ever doing wrong, as if he were her protector, as if . . .

As if she cared deeply for him.

"You ought to have seen the way he skittered out of the house," she was saying, a laugh sailing through her voice. "You'd have thought I caught him stealing cookies instead of spending time with Mrs. White."

"He spoke of her at length yesterday," Mitchell said as he nudged Trip around a hole, remembering the hopeful look in George's eyes as he talked about Mrs. White.

"Did you hear the story of how Arlen and Josie met?"

"Let me guess. He came looking for work, and she fell immediately for his charming ways and good looks?" He slid a gaze over to Lara, unable to conceal a grin.

She laughed. "Now you're making up your own stories."

"Am I?"

That blush he was hoping to see colored her cheeks. "Do you want to hear the story or not?" When he gestured that he did, she continued. "Josie had lost her first husband—a man her father insisted she marry—in a terrible blizzard that killed nearly all the men in town. Pastor Collins was pushing the ladies in town to remarry quickly, which Josie wanted no part of. But George got the idea that marrying again might settle her down, so he sent for a man on her behalf."

Mitchell arched an eyebrow. "George didn't place much value on his own life, did he?"

Lara smiled. "I don't think he thought it through. But Arlen ended up being that man, so it must have worked out. Although he once told me that Josie tried more than once to run him off." She paused. "I always thought it interesting that George was so invested in finding a husband for Josie, and yet he never found a wife for himself."

The answer was obvious to Mitchell. "He never met the right woman."

"Perhaps." She watched him for a second as he kept his eyes on the terrain ahead. "Is that true for you?"

Mitchell nearly choked on his own saliva. Goodness, but this woman could be direct. He slid a gaze toward her. "I suppose it was."

"Was?"

He let her question linger in the air, offering instead a smile before turning to look ahead again.

"Well, you know all about my family. My little brothers, my parents, and everyone here. And I still know nothing of yours, save that you have one."

"Had." The bright day felt a little colder, a little darker.

"I'm sorry." The hitch in her voice made him look up. Her pretty blue eyes were somber, and empathy radiated from her. He imagined that if they weren't on horseback, she might reach over and take his hand.

"I understand if you don't want to talk about them, but I'd love to hear your memories if you care to share them."

It was possibly the nicest thing anyone had ever said to him. She didn't ask how he'd lost them. She only wanted to know what he'd loved about them.

The pain seemed to split in half, and up from the middle, like a volcano on some faraway island, the memories came pouring out. The good ones, the ones that made life on the ranch feel so familiar.

"One Christmas," he said hesitantly. "My father made my two youngest sisters—they were twins—a little rocking horse. You ought to have seen my other sister when they opened it. She was only about a year older than them, and she broke down in wails and tears. We all thought she'd gotten over it, but the next day the rocking horse disappeared. Mama found it later on, hidden in the corner of Becky's bedroom, covered over with quilts. When Mama told her she needed to apologize for taking it, Becky crossed her arms and asked for an apology for Mama giving her two little sisters."

Lara laughed. "I think I would've liked Becky."

"You would have. I wish . . ." Mitchell trailed off. He'd never put those thoughts into words before, the ones that covered the gaping hole in his heart where his family had once lived.

Lara looked at him, clearly waiting for him to finish the thought.

It would be easy to swallow it, keep it right where he had for ten years now. But it pushed to be spoken, and maybe . . . Maybe it would help to lay it bare. Let it out in the world instead of keeping it hidden inside.

"I wish I'd been able to know her grown up. Her and my brother and the twins." He swallowed. There it was, part of his very soul lifted out for all to see.

Except it wasn't all the world. It was only Lara.

And she looked at him now without pity, but with his own sadness reflected in her eyes. "How old was she when . . ." She swallowed. "I'm sorry, you don't need to answer that."

He gave her a reassuring smile. "Twelve. Calvin was fourteen and the twins were eleven."

"She was just shy of Hannah's age," Lara said.

Mitchell nodded. More than once he'd looked at Hannah and thought of Becca, though the two looked nothing alike. "The world would have been a better place with her in it."

"Did you get along with Calvin, or were you like Belle and me when we were younger, always picking on each other?" Lara asked. She was trying to draw out the happy memories, and oddly, he didn't mind.

So he told her of Calvin, and of the mischievous twins. And then of his sweet but fiery Mama and his Papa, the man he'd always admired most in the world. She listened and laughed at the funny parts and asked gentle questions.

Not once did she ask how they'd died.

And yet she was the only one he wished to know.

"It was a fever," he finally said as they passed a stand of browned evergreens. "That's what took them. I was the only one to survive." He shifted in the saddle and stopped the horse. "I've never spoken of it. I think . . . I felt guilty over it for years."

She nodded. "I can see how."

He knew better now, of course. There was no controlling an illness that did as it pleased. But somehow, the simple act of telling her left an ease in his soul. As if that guilt had still clung in tattered threads, and now it had been wiped away.

"Lara, I . . .Thank you." It was all he could think to say.

Her horse danced next to his. He reached out and laid a hand on her arm. She let go of the reins and turned her arm, letting his hand slide down to hers.

"That's the first time anyone has thanked me for asking too many questions." Her smile was sweet, but something sad sat behind it.

Mitchell let go of her hand and reached up to brush a thumb over the corner of her lips.

Her eyes closed. It would be so easy to lean forward, to close the distance between them.

To kiss her.

A small sigh escaped her lips, and Mitchell came undone. He grazed his hand across her cheek and moved forward, just a little, until his lips were less than an inch away from hers. Her breath caressed his face, and he wanted to keep this moment alive forever.

His eyes closed—and a movement sounded from somewhere behind him.

Chapter Thirteen

Lara gasped as Mitchell snapped around. The moment they'd shared was gone, broken by whatever—or whoever—was rustling through the trees and mostly dead brush beside them.

"What is it?" She practically breathed the words, not wanting to alert whatever it was to their presence.

Mitchell didn't answer, but he rested a hand on the holster at his hip as he urged Trip forward toward the trees. Then he stopped and they sat in silence for several long moments.

No sound came from the trees, and finally, Mitchell dropped his hand and gestured at Lara to begin riding back toward the ranch.

"Must have been an animal. Maybe a fox or a coyote," he said when they were well enough away from the trees. But despite his words, he turned to look behind them every few minutes as if he didn't trust his own explanation.

"I haven't brought Arlen and George their meals," Lara said. The fear had worn away, and now she worried over how hungry they must be.

"We ought to have seen them by now. They most likely headed back toward the west. Or back home." He glanced behind them again, even though the copse of trees was far in the distance by now.

"Is everything all right?" Lara asked quietly.

"It's fine." His words were spoken in a tone that was shorter than usual. Lara wanted to ask more, try to figure out what had spooked him so, but she forced herself to keep her questions to herself.

Perhaps Mitchell worried that the man who had come after her had returned. But that was so unlikely—even the sheriff himself had said so. And besides, the noise they'd heard had been low to the ground, more animal-like than anything a person could cause, unless he'd been crawling on all fours.

So instead of worrying, Lara decided to be flattered by the way Mitchell held such concern for her. She let her gaze wander toward him again. He sat a horse as if he'd grown up in the saddle. She tried to imagine him learning as a child, dark hair wild in the wind as he galloped up a hill, whooping and shouting as only a boy could. Maybe his brother rode with him, or his father.

Her heart ached as she thought of his family. No wonder he held such sadness behind his eyes. Lara thought she would too, if she'd lost everyone she loved.

But there was something else too. He'd said as much out by the water drill that night Belle had found them. That thing he'd done. What could it be? She hated that something could bother him so.

"I'm glad you're here," she said, seemingly out of nowhere, desperate to make him smile again.

The worry seemed to slip from his eyes. "I'm glad I'm here too."

"Want to race me back?" She wanted to see him push against the wind, ride as if there was nothing else to worry about in the world.

It worked. His face crinkled into a smile. "I never turn down a challenge." And without another word, he urged Trip into a gallop.

"Neither do I, Mitchell King," Lara shouted after him as she nudged Murray to catch up.

They arrived, winded and rumpled, back at the house only to find everyone gathered around the water drill.

"Water!" Dot yelled to them as she and Joseph ran toward the horses.

"Mr. Chapman found *water*!" Joseph's eyes were as big as the full moon. "Under the ground!"

Lara leapt off Murray, and together, she and Mitchell joined the family gathered around the drill.

And sure enough, water was burbling from the hole the drill had dug.

"Well, I'll be," Mitchell said. "It worked."

Lara was smiling too big to tease him about how certain he'd been about the water. Belle and Hannah clung to each other, laughing each time the water spurted up from the ground. And Lara didn't think she'd ever seen Arlen so filled with joy as he wrapped an arm around Josie.

"We're going to make it," he said, disbelief lacing his voice. "We're going to make it."

Dot shrieked and grabbed hold of Lara's hands. Lara tossed Murray's reins to Mitchell and danced with her little cousin in a circle. She'd never felt so much like celebrating in her life.

"Mama! Water!" Joseph sprinted to the back porch where George carried Isabel in his arms.

Lara shot a glance at Mitchell and grinned. George was truly head over heels for Isabel. He set her gently onto one of the chairs on the porch and then stayed nearby instead of joining in the celebration down by the drill.

Dot pulled Belle and Hannah into their circle, and together, they danced around and around. Lara didn't think anything could feel so good as this—her family, joyful and filled with hope after so long and Mitchell's eyes on her as he grinned.

Not a thing could ruin this moment. And for once, every worry Lara had seemed far, far away.

Chapter Fourteen

Mitchell had never thought water could taste so good. Glass after glass they drank that afternoon and all through supper. Afterward, they gathered on the back porch and listened to the sound of the water gurgling several feet below ground.

Lara sat on the stairs with her back against a post, Belle opposite her and the children down below, pointing out stars and constellations. Arlen and Josie had turned in a while ago, and George was inside, reading to Isabel while she worked on baby clothing for Josie. Mitchell leaned back in his chair, closed his eyes, and tried to think of another more perfect moment.

This entire day had been memorable. From nearly kissing Lara to finding the water to this still, peaceful time on the porch.

The only thing that had marred it was the rustling in the bushes.

It had been an animal. Of that, Mitchell was absolutely certain. But it had set him on edge.

He still couldn't place the man who had attacked Lara. He wondered if perhaps he'd imagined the similarity to someone he'd known or had met. The man's image seemed to blur in his mind now, mixed in with his time in Denver and the men he'd worked with.

Denver.

He blew out a breath, trying to keep his mind on the good in front of him. Lara, laughing in delight at something Joseph had said. The happy chatter of the two girls. The water burbling away, refreshing and full of promise.

But try as he might, Denver would always be there in the back of his mind.

He'd done wrong, and he'd admitted it. Then he'd saved Clarkson's life by telling them everything. He'd done a *good* thing—that was what he'd told himself over and over. No matter that it had helped him too. It had set him free rather than leaving him to rot in a prison somewhere.

Then why did he feel so badly about it?

And then there was Lara. Determined, curious Lara who wanted to know everything about him. If she knew about his time in Denver, she'd likely ask Arlen and Josie to toss him back out into the road.

But if this . . . whatever it was between them was going somewhere, shouldn't he tell her?

The thought made his stomach churn.

His gaze landed on Lara, who watched him quietly. She stood and took the chair next to his while Belle listened patiently to Joseph's jokes.

"It looks as though you have something on your mind," she said.

Mitchell said nothing. It was as if she could read his thoughts. "Nothing more than I had earlier."

"Hmm." She didn't believe him. That much was clear from the set of her jaw and the way her eyelids narrowed. "When you were thinking of your family, you looked more sad than worried. And when we heard that movement in the trees, you looked ready to fight. This is something else."

"It's nothing to cause concern," he said. And it was the truth. It was all in the past. Clarkson and the other men were in prison. He'd paid his price. No one was coming for him.

She said nothing for a moment. "When I met you, I thought I saw something in your eyes. Something . . . dangerous, I suppose. I don't know what it is, Mitchell, but I think it has something to do with whatever it is that you have on your mind."

He gritted his teeth. Her curiosity would be his undoing if she kept pushing. It was sweet—up to a point. If she pressed, she'd learn things she shouldn't.

And that was not something he'd let happen. Not when everything he held here was on the line—including her.

"Some things are best left in the past, Lara." He stood abruptly and stepped over the children and Belle on the stairs. He needed air, needed space, needed a moment to remind himself there was no reason that any of it should ever surface here.

This wasn't Denver. And he wasn't that man anymore.

Chapter Fifteen

The Wendler children—all seven of them—swarmed the post and telegraph office. Dot, Hannah, and Joseph fell in with them and the Landrys' only son at once.

"Out!" Celia Wendler yelled over the chaos. "Out with all of you!"

The children tumbled out the door of the main room, heading toward what Lara hoped was the back door and not Faith Landry's carefully kept rooms.

"I'll keep an eye on them," Belle said, following the kids out the door.

"Oh, my goodness, listen," Celia said.

Lara listened . . . and didn't hear a thing. She glanced at Faith, who raised her eyebrows at her sister Celia.

"There is nothing to hear," Faith said as she sorted through a stack of mail.

"Exactly." Celia grinned. "This never happens at home unless it's the dead of night."

Lara could only imagine, with all of those children. It was loud enough at their ranch with just Josie's girls and the addition of Joseph. She tried to remember what it was like back in Ohio, with all her younger siblings. She couldn't remember it being that loud—but maybe it was because she'd been a child too.

"Let's see, Josie has a letter, and I know I've set some things aside for her husband and for George." Faith bustled over to a shelf to search while Celia sat in a nearby chair and closed her eyes.

"Here they are." Faith handed her a neat stack of envelopes. "How is Josie? She looked exhausted the last time she was in here."

"I think she's past ready to give birth," Lara replied. Faith was one of Josie's oldest friends, and it had pained her to admit she shouldn't ride into town in her condition. "She doesn't much deal well with not doing as she pleases."

Faith laughed. "I remember that from her other pregnancies. Did you know she came galloping into town when she was about five months along with Hannah? I thought Heather's head might burst when she found out."

That sounded exactly like Josie. "Oh! She would want me to tell you that Mr. Chapman and Mr. Young found water on the property."

Faith clapped her hands together. "Did you hear that, Celia? They have water!" She leaned across the counter to whisper to Lara. "I'm trying to convince my sister that she and Jack need to take the financial assistance that Pastor Collins mentioned so they can have the drill come out to their farm. But they're being stubborn."

"I heard that," Celia said without opening her eyes. "And it isn't me you have to convince. It's Jack. He's certain we can raise the money on our own."

"In approximately ten years," Faith said under her breath.

Lara chatted a little longer with the sisters before leaving to accomplish her other task in town. She left the mail with Belle, who was enjoying playing mother to the eleven children under her care behind the post office. Lara was certain that whenever Belle found the right man to marry, she'd wind up with an entire brood of babies, just like Celia.

The town was still dry and dusty, although the well in the park was a welcome change. Folks lined up to collect water in buckets and cups, chatting happily among themselves. It had been some time since everyone in Last Chance had been so cheerful.

Lara found herself walking with an extra bounce in her step to the library. The building that now served as the library used to be the schoolhouse, when there were enough children in town to warrant a schoolhouse. It was one of Lara's favorite places in town, made even more so by the kindly older woman who ran it.

"Good afternoon, Mrs. Payne," she said when she spied the lady at a table with a stack of books.

"Miss Cummings!" The librarian's eyes sparkled with joy. "It's good to see you in town again."

"Did you hear that we found water?"

"Well, that is a blessing." She stood from behind the table. "Now, were you wanting the newspapers? I have one from Omaha and one from Denver. New ones came with the stage yesterday, so you can take these older copies with you. Give that cousin of yours something to read while she waits for that baby."

Lara followed her across the small room, deciding not to mention that she was the one who devoured the newspapers before anyone else. The others enjoyed paging through and reading an article here and there, but Lara read them front to back, every single line.

Mrs. Payne handed her the papers, and Lara thanked her. Outside, she waved at Mrs. Collins, the pastor's wife, before walking back toward the post and telegraph office. The newspapers under her arms were like beacons, calling her to them, and Lara finally gave in.

She held one of them—the one from Denver—out in front of her as she strolled, letting her eyes skim the headlines. There was so much information packed into these words, everything from the latest happenings in Washington, DC to an opera singer touring California. Lara reread each headline, trying to determine where she would start once she was able to sit down at home and read more.

Just as she reached the last headline, the strangest feeling came over her. It felt as if someone was watching her. Lara placed the paper under her arm again and looked around, expecting to see someone she knew.

But only a handful of people were about—a gentleman headed toward her a block away, and a small family across the road. Lara turned, still trying to put a finger on the feeling she had, and that's when she saw him.

A man of medium stature walked several yards behind her. He was unremarkable in every way save for how he watched her. This was Last Chance, the town where she'd felt comfortable for the past two and a half years. She stopped and was just about to call to the man to see what he needed when she remembered the fellow who had grabbed her back by the road to the ranch.

Lara wrenched her mouth closed. Was he another one to watch out for?

Her heart jumped as the man stopped too. He raised his hat, gave her a smile that elicited shivers up and down her arms, and then turned and walked back the other direction.

Lara watched him a moment, wanting to ensure he disappeared down the road, before letting out a ragged breath and dropping a hand to her chest.

Was she being silly? The man was positively respectful in the way he lifted his hat. He didn't speak to her, much less come after her. He was likely just someone new in town who had lost his way.

Still, Lara's heart didn't slow as she made her way across the road to the post and telegraph office. Something about him and the way he looked at her didn't sit right with her.

And all she wanted to do was get back to the ranch as soon as possible.

#####

It wasn't until later that night that Lara found time to sit with a lamp and the newspapers. She'd shared the one from Omaha with Isabel, who seemed just as curious to learn what was happening around the country and the world as Lara was.

The children were asleep, and most everyone had turned in for the night when Arlen passed by the dining room and reminded her not to stay up all night with the newspaper. Lara promised she wouldn't—after all, a few hours would hardly be the entire night. And there was so much to catch up on!

She spent a few minutes reading a good, long article about a motor race between automobiles in Europe that left her breathless. She turned the page to finish it, but her eyes fell to a sketch at the bottom of the page.

Lara drew in a breath and ran her fingers over the sketch. A man, plain as plain could be, stared back at her.

He looked exactly like the fellow who had been walking behind her in town.

Swallowing hard, Lara read the headline to the short article that accompanied the image.

Buck Clarkson Escapes Prison.

Lara's stomach lurched. It couldn't be the same man, all the way up here in Last Chance . . . Could it? Then again, if one were to escape prison, wouldn't the smartest move be to go somewhere no one would recognize you?

Her fingers shook, and she clenched them into fists as she read the words under the headline. Mr. Clarkson, along with his associates, had apparently been sentenced in Denver for train robbery and murder. He'd been in prison since the prior fall.

And now he was gone without a trace.

Lara looked at the image again. It could be of anyone, she tried to tell herself. But the artist's work was very good, and the resemblance was uncanny.

She stood, unable to remain seated any longer. So many thoughts on what could have happened filled her mind. But they hadn't, thankfully. He'd gone his way—once he'd seen that she noticed him.

What would have happened if she hadn't turned around?

Perhaps he would have simply stolen her reticule and run off. Or perhaps . . . Images of the blond man who had taken hold of her by the road ran through her mind. What was happening in Last Chance? Never before had Lara felt a reason to be afraid here.

She closed the newspaper. *Denver*. That was where Mitchell had come from. Perhaps he knew of this man.

Lara gathered up the newspaper and stepped outside. Striding toward the bunkhouse—and hoping no one was awake to see her doing something so scandalous—she hoped Mitchell could set her mind at ease.

Chapter Sixteen

The knock came, insistent and hard. And when Mitchell took the time to set aside the knife and the little duck he was carving for Joseph, the knock came again, even more insistently.

Something was wrong.

Thinking of a hundred different possibilities from fire to illness, Mitchell crossed quickly to the door and pulled it open.

Lara looked back at him, a newspaper in her hand and her eyes wide.

"Lara?" He almost didn't believe it was her standing there. What would possess her to come down here so late at night?

"Please, may I come in?" she said, an urgent tone to her voice.

Mitchell looked behind him, as if somehow expecting to see someone else in this empty bunkhouse. "That really isn't the best—"

She waved a hand at him. "I know it's improper, but I didn't come down here to kiss you."

And that rendered him speechless. He wondered if he were the one blushing for once. "Well, I'm sorry to hear that," he said, scrambling to regain his composure.

A flicker of amusement appeared in her otherwise serious face. "I need to speak with you, and I don't wish to awaken anyone."

Mitchell glanced past her toward the darkened house. "All right. But we're leaving the door open." It wouldn't matter, not if Arlen or George—or, heaven forbid, Josie—came down here to investigate, but it made him feel somewhat better about the situation.

Lara pushed past him to the table in the middle of the room. She ran a finger over the half-carved duck and smiled before opening the newspaper and setting it flat on the table. She pointed at something toward the bottom. "This is what I wanted to show you."

Mitchell tucked his hands into his pockets and joined her. Her finger pointed at an article near the bottom of the page next to an image of a man.

A man who looked far too familiar.

Mitchell tried to keep his expression impassive as his eyes raked over the artist's rendition of Buck Clarkson—a man he never thought he'd see again.

A man who had now escaped prison.

He couldn't fully comprehend the words in the article, but the gist of it was bright as day. Clarkson had escaped. Clarkson, who thought Mitchell was the one responsible for his sentence.

Get a hold of yourself, King. Clarkson didn't know where he'd gone. He was a good two hundred miles from Denver.

"When was this paper printed?" He reached for the corner and turned the page back.

"A few weeks ago? It doesn't matter," Lara said, twisting her hands in front of her.

Exactly three weeks ago, according to the date on the front page. Three weeks for Clarkson to ask around about him.

And then something else occurred to him.

His eyes found Lara's. "Why are you showing me this?" She couldn't know. It was impossible. The article didn't mention his name.

She bit down on her lip, and he thought he saw fear cross her face like a shadow. "He was in town. I'm certain of it. And he . . . Mitchell, I think he was following me."

The world seemed to swirl around him, loud and silent, bright and dark, all at once. He gripped the edge of the table and tried to force his mind to function.

Facts. He needed facts. And then he could make a decision.

"Tell me what he looked like," he said to Lara.

She tilted her head, as if she wasn't entirely certain why he was asking when the man's image was right there in the newspaper. "Not like much of anything, really. Brown hair, not very tall but not short, just . . . like any other man."

That was Clarkson's particular talent—blending into any place, any scenario. He was just as much at home in a first-class railroad car as he was among the men guarding the payload in the last car.

"Did he threaten you?" he asked.

"Not at all," Lara replied. "When I realized he was behind me, he simply stopped, raised his hat, and turned around. I . . . to be honest, I'm not sure he *was* following me. It was only a feeling I had. Maybe it was because I'm still a little spooked from what happened down by the road—"

"You were right to be wary." He glanced down at the paper. It had been Clarkson. He felt it deep inside. It was far too coincidental for a stranger who just happened to look like him to be the one who'd followed Lara.

He pushed down the urge to toss a saddle on Trip and ride into town, to yank Clarkson out of whatever boardinghouse he'd found and show him exactly how he felt about him scaring Lara.

"Mitchell?" Her voice was quiet, threaded through with concern.

He pulled his gaze from the newspaper and back up to her. For the hundredth time, he was struck with how beautiful she was. That red hair was like a fire that never went out and the soft planes of her face begged for his touch.

Mitchell swallowed hard, trying to press those thoughts to the back of his mind. This was all too good to be true. He should have known that the second he accepted the job here.

"It was him, wasn't it?" she asked.

He nodded once, and then leaned over to fold up the paper. "You ought to get back up to the house before you're missed."

"It's the dead of night. No one will be missing me."

He could feel her eyes on him, but he didn't look up, opting instead to crease the edges of the newspaper.

"Should we go to see the sheriff in the morning?" she asked. "I worry about the folks in town with this Mr. Clarkson about."

It wasn't the people in town who needed to be worried. It was him—and everyone he associated with here.

"Go on back up to the house, Lara," he said in a measured voice.

But she didn't move. He should have known she wouldn't obey without asking twenty-seven questions first.

"Not until you tell me what's wrong." She paused, glancing down at the creased newspaper in his hands. "Do you know him? This Mr. Clarkson?"

Mitchell felt as if he'd swallowed a baseball. She didn't need to know. She *couldn't* know.

"Mitchell . . ." Her voice trailed off as she bit down on her lip. "You're worrying me. Was he following me for a reason beyond simply being where I was at the time? Are we in danger? Should I wake Arlen—"

"No," he said sharply as he smacked the paper back down on the table.

Lara jumped just slightly, and he felt awful for scaring her.

Although maybe she *should* be scared of him. That would make the inevitable much easier.

He ran his hands through his hair, trying to think. When he looked up again, she still watched him, her blue eyes edging on irritated.

"Are you going to tell me what's going on?" she asked. "Or should I ride back into town, find Mr. Clarkson, and ask him myself?"

He reached out and gripped her shoulders. Her eyes went wide. He had her attention.

"Lara, no matter what, do *not* go seeking that man out. Do you understand me?"

She frowned. "Then are you going to tell me about him?"

He held her gaze for a moment, his hands still on her shoulders. Then he dropped them, took hold of her arm, and pulled her toward the door. "Go back up to the house. Now." He didn't even bother asking her to keep this information to herself. It didn't matter, not now.

"No." She crossed her arms the second she was outside and he let go.

He rubbed a hand across his face. She wouldn't listen to reason. And there was only one other way he could get her to do what he needed at this moment. "Look, you promised me you'd find out more about me. And you have. You went digging, and you resurrected the one thing I never wanted to think of again. So thank you for that, Lara. Go on back up to the house and leave me be."

She dropped her arms, blinking at him as if he'd hit her. His heart lurched as her eyes hardened. "I did no such thing and you know it. If you don't think you can trust me, you're a fool, Mitchell King. I'm the one you can trust more than anyone else in the world." And with that, she did as he'd asked—turned on her heel and marched back up to the house.

He was alone now, as he had been every day before he'd arrived here. This was the second time he thought he'd found family—but unlike the first time, losing this one would hurt.

It would more than hurt. It would gut him.

But there was no other choice, not if he wanted to keep them safe. He'd do whatever it took to make that happen, to keep Clarkson away from them.

Without waiting to change his mind, Mitchell fetched his satchel and began filling it.

Chapter Seventeen

"He's gone." Arlen stood in the doorway to the dining room as Belle served breakfast, a look of surprise creasing his face.

"Gone?" George echoed.

"Trip isn't in the stable, and the bunkhouse is empty."

The table erupted into chatter, but Lara stood. Someone called after her—Josie, perhaps—as she rushed from the room, but she didn't acknowledge them. She ran without stopping across the yard as the morning sun still hung low in the sky.

She blew into the bunkhouse like the wind, her eyes raking the place for evidence that Mitchell had simply just gone for a morning ride.

But Arlen was right. He was gone.

There wasn't even a piece of dirt left to show he'd been there—except . . . Lara picked up the half-carved duck on the table and hugged it to herself.

Why would he have left?

The untamed part of her mind said it was because of her. Because she was too nosy for her own good.

But that wasn't it, no matter what he'd told her to get her to leave the bunkhouse last night. He used that as an excuse because he knew it would hurt her enough to make her leave. And she'd fallen for it.

No, this had nothing to do with her, of that she was absolutely certain. Instead, it had everything to do with that man in town. Mr. Clarkson, the outlaw who'd escaped from prison and had come to Last Chance . . .

Lara set the duck down on the table. No one just happened upon Last Chance, not if they didn't intend to come here. That man was here for a reason.

He was here for Mitchell.

Lara was certain of that. But what connection did an outlaw like Clarkson have to do with Mitchell? She knew it had something to do with whatever it was he'd carried deep inside him. That thing that sat like a somber shadow behind his eyes at times, behind the raw memories of his family.

The part of him he wouldn't tell her about.

Whatever this was, it had to be bad. Which meant that Mr. Clarkson knew exactly who she was when he'd followed her in town yesterday. It hadn't been a mistake at all. It was meant to scare her—and to scare Mitchell.

And it had worked, because now he was gone.

She swallowed a sob that had worked its way up her throat. This wasn't the time to cry. She had to remain strong.

She had to *do* something. But what?

"Lara?"

Lara turned to see Josie standing in the doorway, her hands laying protectively over her stomach.

"Are you all right?" Josie asked as she shut the door behind her. "Belle wanted to come down here, but I convinced her to entertain the children instead." She paused. "I thought that might be for the best."

Lara forced herself to smile at her cousin. She loved Belle dearly, but the last thing she needed was her sister sighing and shaking her head and telling her she'd just known it would come to this. "Thank you."

Josie pursed her lips and looked around the empty room. Her gaze landed on the partially finished duck, and the corner of her lips tugged up. Then she looked at Lara. "He didn't leave willingly, did he?"

Lara wanted to melt into her cousin's arms. Josie knew. She understood. "I don't believe so."

"Do you know why, then? George is beside himself, and Arlen's blaming himself for asking too much of a man he couldn't pay. I finally convinced them to go out and check on the cattle." She paused. "But I doubt his leaving had anything to do with the work."

"It didn't." Lara rested a hand on the little duck. "He loved it here. He said it was like home to him. That we reminded him of his own family."

Josie nodded, not pressing for more but letting Lara speak as she could.

Lara drew in a deep breath. "Yesterday, when I went into town, there was a man I didn't know. It seemed like he was fol-lowing me, but I couldn't tell for certain. So I didn't say any-

thing to you or Belle or anyone. But then last night, I was reading the newspaper from Denver, and I saw him."

"In the newspaper?" Josie asked, wrinkling her brow.

"Yes. There was an artist's rendering. A very good one, too.
It was definitely the man I'd seen in town. He was . . ." She
pulled her hand away from the duck and dug her fingers into
her skirts. "He'd escaped from prison in Colorado."

"Oh, Lara." Josie let out a breath and pulled out one of the
chairs to sit down. "I'm sorry. That had to be terrifying to dis-
cover on your own. I wish you'd woken me."

Lara swallowed. "I know I shouldn't have, but I came down
here. I wanted to show Mitchell, considering he was from Denver and he'd rescued me from that other man on the road. I
thought maybe he might have heard of the man."

Josie nodded, no trace of judgment or reprimand to be
seen.

"And, well . . . Josie, he knew him, the man in the paper.
Mr. Buck Clarkson. He didn't say as much, but the questions
he asked, and the look on his face, and . . . and . . . now he's
gone."

Josie was quiet for a moment. Lara took the chair beside
her, hoping that sitting might calm the nerves that made her
want to go running . . . where? To town? To Denver?

Where had Mitchell gone?

"What was this Mr. Clarkson imprisoned for?" Josie asked.

Lara forced her thoughts back to the present. "Murder, the
newspaper said. Murder and train robbery."

Josie drew in a deep breath and then let it out.

And at that moment, Lara *knew*. Mitchell had been in-
volved in some way with this Clarkson, and the only thing that

made sense was . . . exactly what Clarkson had been convicted of. Robbery.

She closed her eyes and prayed it wasn't murder. She couldn't fathom Mitchell doing something so terrible, so heinous. She refused to believe that until she heard it from his own mouth.

But robbery . . . she could see how a desperate man might fall prey to easy money. A man without a family. And if this Mr. Clarkson had been caught and convicted and Mitchell had not, then . . .

Of course he'd come here. For revenge.

She caught Josie's eye, and just from the look on her cousin's face, she knew Josie had pieced it together too.

"Leaving was the worst thing he could have done. That man will follow him." Josie pushed herself up to standing. "If he'd stayed, Arlen and George would have helped him. *I* would have helped him, if I could. That Mr. Clarkson wouldn't have stood a chance against the four of us."

Lara nodded slowly. "But what do I do now? I can't let him go. I can't let him—" *Walk into a trap*. She couldn't finish the sentence.

Josie glanced around the room as if she might find an answer in the empty corners. "You could saddle up Murray. Go find Arlen and George. Tell them what's happened, and I know they'll go after him."

That would take time. Too much time. "It might be too late by then," Lara whispered. "If he left last night . . ."

Josie shook her head. "He wouldn't have gone at night. It's too dangerous. His horse could have turned an ankle, and you know how much he loves that horse. He would have waited until first light."

"He can't be too far away." Plans swirled and formed in Lara's mind. "I'll go now. Send Belle out to find Arlen and George. They can catch up to me."

Josie ran a hand over her belly. "I should tell you not to do that, but I'd do the same if I were in your shoes. I only wish I could go with you, but this babe won't let me do such things. Come up to the house and I'll give you a pistol. We'll send Belle out right away. Do you know what direction he may have gone?"

Lara pondered the options. He wouldn't have gone into town, and he wouldn't have taken the road that led to Denver.

"East. It's the only way that makes sense."

Chapter Eighteen

The dusty road stretched on, never-ending, eastward toward Grand Platte. If he kept up a good pace, Mitchell figured he could put enough distance between himself and Last Chance that by the time Clarkson realized he was gone, it would be too late.

He only hoped the man wouldn't take out his frustrations on the family he'd left behind.

No. He wouldn't. Clarkson would be too consumed with following him. With getting his revenge on the man he thought had betrayed him.

From Grand Platte, there were a hundred different ways he could disappear. And this time, he'd use an assumed name—one that Clarkson couldn't use to track him down.

Noon came and went, and Mitchell didn't pause to eat. He didn't have much food with him anyway, besides some cheese he'd brought back to the bunkhouse after dinner the night before. He tried not to think of supper at the ranch, made even better now with more water available.

He tried not to think of Arlen and George, disappointed that he didn't stay on.

Tried not to think of the children, who brightened his mood each day.

And he especially tried not to think of Lara.

What was she doing now? Did she think of him? He hoped not. He hoped she understood that he only needed her to leave last night, and that he didn't mean what he'd said about her digging into his past.

Because she hadn't. By all the grace in the world, she'd respected his need to keep the past in the past when he'd asked her, and she'd only teased out what she knew he needed to talk about—his family.

Mitchell's heart ached as Trip trotted along the road. Leaving her was the hardest part of all of this. He hadn't realized how much he'd grown to rely upon those daydreams of them spending a life together, living on the ranch, starting a family.

He hadn't realized how much he loved her.

He squeezed his eyes shut for a moment, trying to push past those thoughts, but it was impossible. They demanded to be heard.

Did she feel the same way about him? Mitchell pressed the reins between his fingers, praying that she didn't. Because if she didn't, then this wouldn't hurt as much for her. And he didn't want her to hurt.

But if she did feel the same way . . . Would she wait for him? A tiny ray of hope bloomed in his chest. If she waited, and Clarkson was caught, he could return.

He frowned. That might happen, but even if Lara forgave him, Arlen and George wouldn't. If they didn't know his past already, they'd find out. And they would never welcome a thief back into their family.

He could explain. Maybe they would listen. Mitchell had come to think of them all as family, so perhaps they felt the same about him. They could help him.

But how could they if he was running away like a coward? He hadn't even gone for the sheriff. He was too embarrassed by his own actions back when he knew Clarkson. He couldn't face the sheriff looking at him like he was nothing more than an outlaw.

It was cowardly. *He* was acting cowardly.

Mitchell drew up the reins, bringing Trip to a halt at the foot of one of the many bluffs that dotted the west Nebraska landscape.

He had two choices: run away or turn around and fight for what he wanted.

The road behind him stretched out long and thin and brown. But unlike the road that led east, this one had hope at the end of it. Acceptance. Family. Love.

Mitchell King was no coward.

And so he nudged Trip back the way he'd come. Back to Last Chance. Back to everything he wanted. And back to everything he needed to put behind him, for once and for all.

Time seemed to drag on as he rode, yet the sun still moved across the sky.

And then, a couple of hours later, two men on horseback appeared on the horizon.

Mitchell took a deep breath, ignored everything in the back of his mind that told him to turn around and run, and continued forward.

He rode right up to Buck Clarkson and a tall man with straw-colored hair, where they waited at the base of yet another bluff. Recognition bloomed in his mind upon seeing the man who had attacked Lara. He couldn't place the man's name, but he'd seen him once or twice with Clarkson back in Denver. Some associate Clarkson wouldn't cut into his usual jobs, but who acted to intimidate folks when Clarkson needed him to. That attack on Lara had been intentional—to scare Mitchell.

Clarkson's lips curved up into the most unfriendly smile Mitchell had ever seen. "Well, if it isn't Mitchell King. Just the man I've been looking for. You remember John Bryce?" He jerked his head toward the tall man.

Mitchell ignored the pretense of civility. "Let's get on with it. Why are you here?" If the man was going to kill him, Mitchell wanted him to say it out loud.

"Always direct. That's why I liked you." Clarkson leaned forward in his saddle as if they were having a friendly conversation. "I'll be direct with you too then. You served me up to the law to save your own skin. And now you're going to pay for it."

Mitchell opened his mouth to tell Clarkson exactly what he thought of that—but he didn't get a chance.

Instead, the sound of a gunshot filled the empty plains around them, echoing off the bluff and sending them all diving for the ground.

Chapter Nineteen

Lara sank back behind the edge of the bluff, willing her hands to stop trembling. That shot had gone wide. But it was probably for the best since she was too nervous to aim properly anyhow.

"Where did that come from?"

"Who's there?"

Neither of the voices belonged to Mitchell. Lara sucked in a breath and peered around the bluff again. All three men were on their feet, each one armed with a revolver and searching for who had shot at them.

She said a quick prayer of thanks that Mitchell appeared to be unhurt, and then aimed the pistol again.

One more shot. That was all she needed. Even if she missed, Mitchell would figure out she wasn't shooting at him. And it would distract the other two men long enough for him to act.

She drew in a breath and then let it out, just as Papa had taught her all those years ago. She hadn't ever been one much for hunting, but thankfully she hadn't completely forgotten how to shoot.

Letting her finger squeeze the trigger, another bullet erupted from the pistol. She drew back immediately to keep from being seen as a yelp sounded from the direction where she'd aimed.

If they didn't know where she was yet, they'd figure it out quickly.

She looked again, around the edge of the rock to see who she'd hit—and then she smiled with satisfaction. The blond giant of a man—the one who had grabbed her at the ranch—was on the ground and gripping his leg.

Clarkson held his pistol aloft, searching along the edge of the bluff. And behind him . . .

Mitchell raised his own gun, aiming it at Clarkson. "Turn around, Clarkson!"

The other man whipped around. "Are you mad? There's someone behind that bluff shooting at us."

"Doesn't seem they're shooting at me," Mitchell replied. "Throw down your weapon."

"Not a chance." Clarkson looked behind him, toward where Lara hid behind the bluff.

"I'm warning you," Mitchell said. "I don't want to shoot you, not after I kept you alive. But I will if I have to."

"You mean after you threw me over to the law to save your own neck?"

"I saved you from the noose. You're too angry to see past your own nose, but me telling them exactly what happened bought you your life."

Clarkson laughed, the noise ricocheting off the bluff. "You're afraid. That's all you've ever been. Afraid."

"Put down the gun," Mitchell repeated.

"I don't—" The sound of another bullet cut off Clarkson's response.

Lara jumped, a shriek escaping her lips despite her best efforts to keep it in. Clarkson flew around, searching for the sound she'd made, but it wasn't him who drew her attention.

It was Mitchell, who clutched his arm, his pistol on the ground. A wisp of smoke curled from the blond man's gun. They'd forgotten about him.

And now he'd shot and disarmed Mitchell.

Lara dug her fingers into the soft stone of the bluff as Clarkson took a step toward where she hid. Her other hand clung to the revolver.

"Watch him," Clarkson threw back at the other man, who, despite his injury, held his gun on Mitchell. "I'm going to suss out whoever's behind that bluff." He raised his gun. "Come on out!"

Lara held her breath and didn't move an inch. She could just barely see him as she peered around the edge of the stone.

"Sounded like a woman," the blond man said.

"You send your lady after us, King?" Clarkson said with a dead-sounding laugh. "I got a good look at her in town. All that red hair. Didn't look like she could harm an ant."

"She shot Bryce, didn't she?" Mitchell said, pain lacing his voice. Lara could just make out a tinge of red soaking through his shirt.

"Lucky shot," Clarkson replied. "Come on out, girlie," he shouted toward her as he gripped his pistol with both hands.

"Give up now and I might let your man die quickly." He chuckled at that as Lara shuddered.

She could shoot again. She had enough bullets. But then that Bryce fellow could shoot Mitchell.

Perspiration dripped down the sides of her forehead. What could she do? What would Josie do in this situation?

A shot rang out.

Chapter Twenty

Despite the fire in his arm, Mitchell ducked when the shot flew past Clarkson—and barely missed Bryce. It hadn't come from the person behind the bluff. The angle wasn't right.

But wherever it had come from, it had distracted Bryce long enough to allow Mitchell to scoop his own pistol up from the ground. It felt odd in his left hand, but he didn't have long to think about that. When Bryce turned back around, Mitchell aimed it at him.

"Who was that?" Clarkson roared at the sky. He turned this way and that, revolver held in his outstretched arms, searching for the source of the latest gunshot.

Mitchell didn't pay him much mind. At least Bryce couldn't up and shoot him now that Mitchell also aimed at him.

Another shot echoed off the bluff. It was close enough to make Clarkson's horse dance sideways.

"Clarkson," Bryce croaked from where he sat on the ground. When Clarkson glanced back at him, he nodded at the road toward the west.

Mitchell followed his gaze and saw the most welcome sight he thought he'd ever seen.

A cloud of dust rose in the distance, but he could just make out men on horseback. Multiple men on horseback.

Mitchell jerked his gaze toward the bluffs. The person hiding behind them and— A glint of silver shone from atop the lowest bluff. There was a second person up there.

They'd come for him. Arlen, George . . . It couldn't be Lara, as Clarkson had thought. Could it? He didn't know who it was, but they were there. And those riders headed toward them. She'd somehow alerted the sheriff.

"It's too late," he said to Clarkson. "They're coming for you."

Bryce shook his head and laid down his gun. "I'm done with this."

But Clarkson wheeled around. Mitchell recognized that fire in his eyes. It was the same look he'd seen just before they'd been apprehended after trying to rob the train leaving Denver.

Clarkson was a man with nothing to lose.

He leveled his pistol at Mitchell.

Mitchell didn't have a moment to think past the instinct to save himself. He shot before Clarkson did.

The man fell, landing in a heap of dust on the ground. Mitchell sunk to his knees, lightheaded from the pain in his arm, but not daring to drop his pistol.

He caught a flash of pink in the corner of his eye, but he didn't avert his gaze from Clarkson.

"Mitchell!" Lara's voice, insistent and oh, so, so welcome, penetrated his mind, and then she was there, beside him, pulling his injured arm away to examine it.

"King." Another voice, male this time, came from behind him. "You can lower your gun. I've got him."

Arlen came into sight, just off to the side, his shotgun aimed at Clarkson, who was beginning to stir on the ground. George was right behind him.

Mitchell blinked. They were here. All of them. And Clarkson had been right. One of the shooters was a woman.

Lara.

She'd come for him, and she'd brought Arlen and George—and half the town, it appeared to be from the men just beginning to pull up nearby. Bryce raised both of his hands while Clarkson moaned from the ground.

Mitchell finally lowered his pistol. "Lara," he said, still in disbelief as she gently let go of his hurt arm.

"I'm here." She laid a hand over his cheek and gave him an encouraging smile. "You didn't have to do this alone."

He shook his head, still trying to piece together what had happened.

But she was right. He wasn't alone—and he never had been.

He had a family.

Chapter Twenty-one

"Sit down, or I'll send Josie out here to keep an eye on you." Lara set down the cup of coffee she'd brought Mitchell on the front porch and popped a hand onto her hip.

He stopped, halfway to standing, and then sat again. "Yes, ma'am."

She pulled up a chair to sit next to him.

Mitchell picked up the steaming cup. He took a sip and closed his eyes. "Didn't think I'd ever taste coffee with clean water again."

Lara smiled. "Everything is better with water." And it was the truth. The ranch was slowly coming back to life. George and Arlen had been up half the night again, but this time discussing plans for the future instead of worries about failure.

Mitchell set the cup back down and adjusted his arm, grimacing.

"The doctor said you ought to be lying down," Lara said as Belle went chasing after Joseph, who was chasing Shep across the yard. "Want me to help you back inside?"

Mitchell eyed her. "Don't think you can be ordering me around once I'm all healed up."

"I'm *not* ordering you around. I'm simply reiterating what the doctor said." She gave him her most angelic smile. "Besides, you ought to have seen how Josie tormented Arlen when he sliced open his leg last summer. You'd have thought he was on the verge of death with the way she kept after him."

That made Mitchell look even more pained. Lara bit her lip to keep from laughing. In truth, she was just so happy he was here with her—all in one piece—that she would have tolerated him turning somersaults in the yard with Joseph so long as he wasn't bleeding.

A warmth covered the hand she had rested on the arm of the chair. She looked down to see Mitchell's good hand covering hers. She turned her hand over and laced her fingers through his. She would never get enough of this simple, reassuring gesture.

He was here. Arlen and George had welcomed him back instead of running him off. And he cared for her.

"The sheriff sent word that Clarkson passed on before they could send him back to Denver," Mitchell said quietly.

Lara glanced up at him. "Are you all right?" She couldn't imagine knowing she had taken a man's life, even if it was to protect her own. Her heart hurt for him.

"I will be, once I sit with it for a while." He caught her eyes. "I'll say that I'm grateful this means he'll never bother us again."

Us. His words made Lara feel warm inside. The future. *Their* future. As soon as they'd returned to the ranch, Mitchell spoke haltingly to her of his past while they waited for the doctor to arrive. He'd told her of feeling alone, desperate for friends, and uncertain of anything after losing his family. He'd drifted along for a while, working jobs as he'd found them for a few years before finally landing in Denver. And there, he'd filled the empty place inside with people he thought were friends. People like Clarkson.

But they weren't friends, and Mitchell had found himself in too deep with them before he understood that. Choosing to leave was an impossible decision. He'd felt as if he was betraying the only people to show him kindness since his family. He weighed the decision—until it was made for him.

They were caught just as they attempted to rob yet another train. Clarkson shot a man acting as a guard, and while Mitchell and the others faced charges of robbery, Clarkson was looking at something much more serious. And so when the state offered to withdraw all of the charges against Mitchell and to reduce Clarkson's sentence from death to a lifetime in prison if Mitchell told them everything that they'd done, he agreed.

He'd saved Clarkson's life.

After he told Lara, he repeated the entire story to George and Arlen and had offered to move on as soon as he was well enough.

They wouldn't hear of it.

And so here he was, with her. With them.

Lara squeezed his hand. "Are you in very much pain?"

"It's better than it was. But I'll be glad when I have both my arms again."

"So you can ride and mend fences and search out stray cattle?" she teased.

"Oddly enough, yes. I miss the work. But there's this girl I know, and I'd like to wrap her up in both my arms again too." He gave her a mischievous grin.

"Oh, I don't know that Josie would much care for that," she said, looking up at him sideways.

Mitchell shook his head, still smiling. "You know, Lara, there's something I've been meaning to ask you. I've been trying to wait for the right moment, but time alone is something that's hard to come by around here."

As if to prove his point, Belle, Joseph, and the dog raced by again before disappearing around the side of the house.

Lara laughed. "With eight other people in this house, I can't imagine that."

"So I'm going to ask you now." He shifted in the chair as far as his hurt arm would let him. "I love you, Lara Cummings. I love everything about you—your bravery, your heart, your stubbornness, and yes, your curiosity."

Lara pulled in a breath. "I . . . I love you too, Mitchell." It felt so good to finally say that out loud. "I was so afraid I'd lost you when you left."

He held her gaze. "I'll never leave you again. I promise that."

Tears stung her eyes, and she blinked them away, focusing instead on Mitchell's dear, wonderful face and the reassuring way he held her hand.

"If I could lift my other arm, I'd wipe those away for you," he said with a smile. "So just imagine me doing that, all right?"

Lara laughed, using her own hand to brush away the few tears that had leaked out.

"I want to stay here—with you—forever. I love this ranch, I love this family, I love you. I want to have a life with you. A family of our own." He paused, his eyes tracing her face. "Will you marry me, Lara?"

The words caught in her throat. So instead, she nodded, and then she threw her arms around his neck, taking care not to jostle his arm. He wrapped his good arm around her, and little Joseph giggled at them from somewhere beyond the porch steps.

Lara pulled away, laughing, and then—heedless of the family she knew was watching her now—leaned forward again to kiss her soon-to-be-husband. Mitchell raised his hand to the back of her head, and Lara vaguely heard Belle shoo Joseph along.

They were alone again, for a moment, at least, and Lara lost herself in Mitchell's kiss.

He pulled away for just a second. "I could do this all day."

"I'll count on that, then," she said with a grin before he claimed her lips again. And this time, she lost track of everything except for him.

Her husband. Her family.

Epilogue

October 1895

The flowers were all wrong for a wedding.

Belle frowned at them, trying to arrange them as if shifting a few stems here and there would somehow make them brighter and more cheerful.

"At least we have some flowers," Lara told her sister. "Especially considering how late in the year it is."

"True." Belle set the bouquet aside as a few more people entered the church and took seats. Joseph streaked down the aisle, Hannah chasing after him. "Hmm. I suppose I should help with that."

Lara waved her sister on as Mitchell joined her at the rear of the church.

"Is the bride ready?" he asked.

Lara glanced at Isabel, who was resplendent in a light yellow dress. All she needed was her bouquet, as small and plain as it was. "I believe she is. How about George?"

Mitchell straightened his jacket, looking distinctly uncomfortable in such nice clothing. "He was ready three months ago."

Lara laughed. "Well, in that case, tell Pastor Collins to go ahead and begin."

Belle corralled Joseph and set him on a pew between herself and Josie, who held baby Phillip while giving Joseph a look that clearly said, *Stay put*. Lara handed Isabel the bouquet, and her soon-to-be new cousin smiled nervously at her.

"I never thought I would marry again," she said. "And yet here I am." She glanced down the aisle where George waited for her. "And here he is."

"He's lucky you lost control of that wagon. Else we were all certain he'd die a bachelor," Lara said with a smile of her own. She laid a hand on Isabel's arm and squeezed. "We're so happy to have you join the family."

She took her seat next to Mitchell, and the ceremony began. As Pastor Collins led them in the promises they made to each other, Lara glanced up at her own husband. It had been only a few months since they'd made these same vows.

She laid a hand on her stomach, thinking of the news she had yet to share with him.

Everyone clapped as Pastor Collins pronounced George and Isabel husband and wife. People streamed toward the newly married couple to offer their congratulations. There would be plenty of time to celebrate back at the ranch, and if Lara had to contain her news any longer, she thought she might burst.

"Come with me." She grabbed hold of Mitchell's hand and pulled him to the rear of the church, and out the door.

She stopped in front of the memorial area that held the markers for all the men who had perished in the blizzards so long ago and turned to face her husband.

"What's wrong?" Mitchell asked, concern lacing his features.

"Nothing. Nothing at all." She couldn't stop smiling. "I wanted to say something earlier, when I found out for certain, but you were with George and there was so much to do to get Isabel ready . . . But now they're married and I can finally tell you."

"Tell me what?" He raised his eyebrows, his dark eyes as curious as she imagined hers often were.

Lara bit her lip. "We're having a baby."

He blinked at her.

"Did you hear me? We're having a baby!"

He blinked again, and then his face creased as he shouted in glee. He wrapped his arms around her and swung her around before setting her down quickly.

"That didn't hurt the baby, did it?"

Lara laughed. "No, he—or she—is just fine."

"When?" he asked.

"Sometime next spring. May, most likely, Cecily said this morning."

"A baby." He shook his head. "I'm going to be a father."

Lara wrapped her arms around him. "You'll be the best father."

"A baby," he said again, looking down at her as he rested his hands on her shoulders. "You're incredible, Lara, do you know that?"

She shrugged. "I suppose."

He laughed and then ducked his head to kiss her. Lara leaned into him, drinking in his warmth and his scent. She never knew what she was missing before she met him. Mitchell King was everything she didn't know she needed.

She leaned back, breaking off their kiss. "I'm going to talk to Josie and Isabel, and definitely Celia Wendler, and perhaps a couple of ladies in town. I need to know what's coming. I'm going to find out every little detail."

Mitchell threw back his head and laughed. "I'm not surprised. Just don't pry too much, all right? Not all women might want to tell you every moment of their experiences."

"Me?" Lara pressed a hand to her chest, feigning offense. "I would never do such a thing."

Mitchell moved his hands to her face, his eyes tracing her features. "I hope our child looks exactly like you. Red hair, blue eyes, exactly ten freckles."

"I am *not* freckled, Mr. King. How dare you." She grinned as he laughed again.

"You only have ten freckles because it's October. Two months ago, I counted at least twenty-five."

She narrowed her eyes at him. "It's difficult to remember a hat. And I enjoy the out of doors."

"I love each and every one of those freckles." And he kissed each one to prove it.

Lara sighed and leaned her head against his chest. He tucked her under his chin and they stood like that until the wedding party emerged from the church.

"I suppose we ought to join them," he said.

"In a moment." Lara lifted her head and stood on her tiptoes, claiming his lips for one more kiss.

"The family is waiting," he said against her lips, and she knew he loved using the word *family*. Because he'd truly found one here in Last Chance.

"Let them wait," she said.

And she kissed him again.

Thank you so much for reading! I hope you enjoyed Lara and Mitchell's story. Be sure to keep up with the series because Belle's story is coming in Fall 2022! Don't miss the next book in the Last Chance Brides series, *A Chance for Esther*[1] by Marlene Bierworth. What will happen when Esther falls in love with the man running for sheriff—only to find that he's keeping dangerous secrets?

You might also enjoy reading about how Arlen and Josie met (and that, you can guess, is a story!) in *A Groom for Josie*[2]. Want to read even more of my sweet historical western books? A good place to start is with *Building Forever*[3], the first book in my Gilbert Girls series.

A big thank you goes to those readers who suggested the names for the ranch dogs: Anne, Bev, Billye, Cynthia, Deb, Dolores, Edwina, Judith, Karen H., Karen P., Lana, Laura, Leona, Linda H., Linda W., Lynn, Marie, Mary, MaryEllen, Melanie, Melinda, Mitsu, Pam, Phylis, Priscilla, Raffaela, Sandy, Sharon, Sondra, Susanne, Teresa, Theresa, Tina, Viola, and Virginia.

---

1. *https://www.amazon.com/dp/B09RXY2ZRP*

2. *https://bit.ly/GroomforJosie*

3. *http://bit.ly/BuildingForeverbook*

To be alerted about my new books, sign up here: http://bit.ly/catsnewsletter I give subscribers a free download of *Forbidden Forever*, a prequel novella to my Gilbert Girls series. You'll also get sneak peeks at upcoming books, insights into the writer life, discounts and deals, inspirations, and so much more. I'd love to have *you* join the fun!

Turn the page to see a complete list of my books.

More Books by Cat Cahill

Crest Stone Mail-Order Brides series
A Hopeful Bride[1]
A Rancher's Bride[2]
A Bartered Bride[3]
The Gilbert Girls series
Building Forever[4]
Running From Forever[5]
Wild Forever[6]
Hidden Forever[7]
Forever Christmas[8]
On the Edge of Forever[9]
The Gilbert Girls Book Collection – Books 1-3[10]
The Gilbert Girls Book Collection – Books 4-6[11]
Brides of Fremont County series
Grace[12]

---

1. https://bit.ly/HopefulBride

2. http://bit.ly/RanchersBride

3. https://bit.ly/barteredbride

4. http://bit.ly/BuildingForeverbook

5. http://bit.ly/RunningForeverBook

6. http://bit.ly/WildForeverBook

7. http://bit.ly/HiddenForeverBook

8. http://bit.ly/ForeverChristmasBook

9. http://bit.ly/EdgeofForever

10. http://bit.ly/GilbertGirlsBox

11. https://amzn.to/3gYPXcA

12. http://bit.ly/ConfusedColorado

Molly[13]
Ruthann[14]
Norah[15]
Charlotte (part of the Secrets, Scandals, & Seduction boxset)[16]

Other Sweet Historical Western Romances by Cat

***The Proxy Brides* series**
A Bride for Isaac [17]
A Bride for Andrew [18]
A Bride for Weston[19]

***The Blizzard Brides* series**
A Groom for Celia [20]
A Groom for Faith[21]
A Groom for Josie[22]

***Last Chance Brides* series**
A Chance for Lara[23]

***The Matchmaker's Ball* series**
Waltzing with Willa[24]

---

13. https://bit.ly/DejectedDenver

14. https://bit.ly/brideruthann

15. https://amzn.to/3IyJRuA

16. https://books2read.com/u/4joPNj

17. http://bit.ly/BrideforIsaac

18. https://bit.ly/BrideforAndrew

19. https://bit.ly/BrideforWeston

20. http://bit.ly/GroomforCelia

21. http://bit.ly/GroomforFaith

22. https://bit.ly/GroomforJosie

23. https://amzn.to/3sAj0IV

24. https://bit.ly/WaltzingwithWilla

Westward Home and Hearts Mail-Order Brides series
Rose's Rescue[25]
Matchmaker's Mix-Up series
William's Wistful Bride[26]
Ransom's Rowdy Bride[27]
The Sheriff's Mail-Order Bride series
A Bride for Hawk[28]
Keepers of the Light series
The Outlaw's Promise[29]
Mail-Order Brides' First Christmas series
A Christmas Carol for Catherine[30]
The Broad Street Boarding House series
Starla's Search[31]

---

25. https://bit.ly/RoseRescue

26. https://bit.ly/WilliamsWistfulBride

27. https://amzn.to/3s0Lqwq

28. https://bit.ly/BrideforHawk

29. https://bit.ly/OutlawsPromise

30. https://bit.ly/ChristmasCarolCatherine

31. https://amzn.to/32sQuPS

About the Author, Cat Cahill

A sunset. Snow on the mountains. A roaring river in the spring. A man and a woman who can't fight the love that pulls them together. The danger and uncertainty of life in the Old West. This is what inspires me to write. I hope you find an escape in my books!

I live with my family and a houseful of dogs and cats in Kentucky. When I'm not writing, I'm losing myself in a good book, planning my next travel adventure, doing a puzzle, attempting to garden, or wrangling my kids.

Made in United States
Troutdale, OR
09/13/2023

12882199R10082